She could hear the men in the side yard. Alice was right, they never did tire of logging talk....

This evening she let the drone of it flow past her and only perked up to listen when it suddenly stopped dead. What was going on?

Mr. Wicks, the camp superintendent, was marching down the tracks, aiming himself straight toward the group of men. Anybody could tell he was no logger. He had a softness about him that came from pushing a pen instead of a saw, and looked as if he'd been putting away the same prodigious meals as the rest of them without quite burning it all off.

"Boys," he greeted them, nodding. "Don't have to tell you we got tinderbox conditions up here. We'll be sticking to hoot-owl shift, and I want everybody on alert, extra careful."

A low murmur of assent ran through the group.

"Just got word—fire going over at Gales Creek."

"That so?" Storie's father looked over his shoulder to the southeast.

Mr. Wicks nodded. "Some little family show. What I hear, they'll get her licked. Still, let's take it as a warning."

The men shifted uneasily, a couple of them hooking thumbs in their red suspenders and craning back to scowl at the sky.

Storie sat up cross-legged and sniffed the air. Was that smoke she smelled? And just how far away was Gales Creek?

FIRE
ON THE
WIND

LINDA CREW

Published by
Bantam Doubleday Dell Books for Young Readers
a division of
Bantam Doubleday Dell Publishing Group, Inc.
1540 Broadway
New York, New York 10036

ISBN: 0-440-21961-2

RL: 5.2

Reprinted by arrangement with Delacorte Press

Printed in the United States of America

April 1997

10   9   8   7   6   5   4   3   2   1

For my daughter,
Mary Faye Crew,
with love

ACKNOWLEDGMENTS

For assistance on this project, I would like to thank Blanche Casey Evernden, Rozel Hoselton, Molly Gloss, Martha Whiteside, William Welch, Jan Komar, Gretchen Olsen, Sue Shumway and my brother, Bob Welch; Robb Wilson of the Columbia County Historical Museum, Larry Fick and George Martin of the Oregon State Forestry Department in Forest Grove, Mike Kinch of the Oregon State University Library, and the staffs of the Oregon Historical Society, the Corvallis Public Library, the Forest Grove Public Library, the Oregon State Library and the University of Oregon Library.

DISTRICT WARDENS
REPORT ON FIRES

RECORDS SHOW THAT FIRES AND LOSSES IN THE STATE ARE SMALLEST IN MANY YEARS

The most favorable season to date in many years is the report that is sent in to the State Forester's office from all the field men. . . .

—The *Forest Log*
Salem, Oregon
August 1, 1933

A nervous little breeze skittered through the mountain canyons, rattling the leathery leaves of the salal bushes and tickling pale strands of hair across Estora's cheeks. She'd stopped her berry picking when she heard the first shout. Now she shaded her eyes to squint across the abandoned railroad trestle at the Staver boys on the far side.

"Come on, Johnny!" one of them called to her brother. "Highball it on over."

Oh, swell. She'd been hoping her younger

brother could somehow steer clear of this stupid log camp dare game.

The trestle's iron rails were long gone, wooden ties too, taken up as soon as they'd finished logging off this section. All that remained were the timbers bracing the two parallel lines of undergirders across the ravine.

The challenge was to dash clean across one of these fifty-yard stretches of end-to-end logs. An ugly fall if you slipped.

Johnny danced in the dust, loosening up. He glanced at Estora. What? Did he think she'd try to stop him?

Stonily she stared back.

"If you ain't got the guts," Billy hollered, "just figger on playin' with the girls from now on."

Johnny tensed.

"Yellow!"

In this moment of indecision, the hot, sweet smell of ripe blackberries rose around Estora. Daddy'd told them so many times to stay clear of the old trestles. He made out like they were all of them ready to collapse if you so much as touched a toe to the first rotten timber. But it was up here that the berries grew thickest.

Johnny sat and pulled off his shoes.

"You don't have to go worryin' about playin' with the girls," she said to josh him. "There ain't any, remember? Just me."

He stood and glared, refusing to joke.

Estora turned away. A steam donkey engine

shrieked on the next ridge where the Biggs and Bailey Lumber Company was logging its way toward the holdings of Sweetwater Timber, the outfit issuing their father's paycheck. From this distance the engine looked like a toy as Estora watched a newly felled and bucked chunk of tree being hauled by cable up the reddish, fan-shaped gouge in the side of the mountain. From farther beyond, a steam locomotive wailed, probably riding its brakes down a steep switchback grade with another load of logs for the sawmill.

She turned back and found Johnny still sizing up the span.

"You know," she muttered, "you don't *have* to do it."

"Lemme be, Storie."

She sighed. Seemed like boys always *did* have to do it—whatever they were dared. They were like puppets, jerked by strings. Even Jimmy Wicks, the superintendent's son, had taken the trestle dare earlier in the summer. And he read books, for cryin' out loud. She'd figured he had more than sawdust between his ears, but maybe not.

"Well, fine," she said. "Get yourself killed. Then I s'pose I'll be in trouble for it."

He took a deep breath, rose on his toes and lit out, arms pumping.

It wasn't the longest trestle, or anywhere near the highest, because in country this rugged, these logging lines sometimes seemed to have more rails on trestles than anchored to solid mountainsides. They crossed a dozen bigger ones each time they rode the steam train with its shay engine down the mountain into the little hamlet of Brightrain. Still, for a barefoot run, this one was plenty scary.

She shut her eyes. When she opened them, he was halfway across. No, she couldn't look. *Keep going . . . keep going . . .* Finally she heard the cheer erupt. Well, thank God.

Storie watched him get his back slapped. He was one of them now.

"Wanna try it, Storie?" Billy jeered through cupped hands.

She could do it. Daddy always said she was as catty on her feet as any logger. But running the trestle wouldn't make her one of the boys. They'd just change the rules. After all, what good was a manhood test if girls could pass it? When Earlene Bunch had done it last year they'd all gotten mad.

But then, Earlene was different. She'd do anything on a dare, like swiping the dynamite that time and setting it off in the creek, showering fish and debris over half the camp. And now that she'd proved she was worse than all the boys, she was working on grown-woman ways of being bad. People said she was always up at the woods hideaway with one fellow or another. Storie wondered what exactly they did up there at that place above the falls, but she didn't have anybody to ask.

She started down the spur. Let Johnny fall or not fall, she thought. Ain't my lookout. But she couldn't help glancing over her shoulder when she heard the slapping of bare feet on wood behind her. They were running back over the trestle. Johnny was last. She winced, watching his arms pump as he threw himself forward, trusting all to forward momentum.

Ten feet from the end, he looked up and grinned. He'd done it!

Then he slipped.

Storie's bucket clattered in the dust as she dashed back to the ravine's edge. Well, hallelujah. She started breathing again. He'd only fallen six feet.

"Don't tell, Storie!" he was already whimpering.

She slid down to him. What a bloody, sniveling mess.

"Don't tell Dad or he'll whip me!"

She helped him up. "Like to smack you myself, scarin' me like that."

"Aw, Storie—"

"You think I get a kick outta standin' there ready to toss my cookies 'cause you might *die*?"

Sam and Billy were laughing at her. By the time she got Johnny up, they were racing on down the spur, punching each other. You'd have thought the heat would slow them down, but it just seemed to make them ornerier.

Johnny ran a worn flannel sleeve under his nose, trying hard not to cry. Now that he was ten, he'd said he didn't plan to cry ever again.

Storie gave him a grudging hug. "Come on," she said. "Let's go." She snagged the handle of the dumped bucket as they passed it. Still enough for a pie.

Puffs of dust met each footstep on the dirt track of the old railway bed. Only a few weeks ago it had still been muddy along here from the late-spring rains. Then the weather had turned hot and dry, one day after another. Even the moss, usually a damp and spongy carpet over the old downed logs, had dried to a crusty brown. Small forest creatures, scuttling at their approach, rattled the papery leaves of the brush.

Storie licked her lips and thought up a fib about Johnny slipping and scraping his cheek. Mama'd believe it. He was always falling out of trees or tumbling head over heels down steep trails.

"Why'd you have to take Billy's dare anyway?" she said. "Why can't you just say *No, I won't do something stupid just 'cause you tell me to.*"

"Well, Storie," he said, like it was the most obvious thing in the world, "you got to show you ain't scared."

"But ain't some things worth being a-scared of? Here's a ravine. You slip and fall in it, you could die. I believe God means us to be scared, probably to stop us from doin' every fool thing comes into our heads."

"Oh, phooey."

"No, I mean it. Weren't for fear, a kid would

probably get killed the very first day his mama untied him from her apron string."

"But it ain't right to run around scared a things. Mama says so. The *president* says so."

"What are you talkin' about?"

"Mama's always tellin' how he said the only thing we got to fear is fear itself."

"That's talkin' about fearin' to put your money in the bank, Mama says, not daredevilin' stuff."

"Fear's fear," Johnny said loftily. "Same thing."

"Oh yeah? Then here's a dare for you. You march up to Mama and brag how you ran the trestle. Sure! She's gonna say, 'Why, Johnny, that's wonderful! I am just so *pleased* to know you got no fear of fear."

Johnny scowled. And then after a moment he said, "This is probably just one a them things a girl can't ever understand."

She rolled her eyes. She sure couldn't.

"Fire!" The loggers grabbed shovels and scrambled toward the smoke as the cry wailed through Gales Creek canyon. "Fire!"

The log boss's son fought his way down over crisscrossed slash, his heart pounding. What the hell. Last log they were dragging must have shot sparks. *Damn.* Of all the lousy, rotten breaks . . .

But it wasn't so big yet. *Don't panic.* Still campfire size and they were right on it, good men. They'd lick this quick. *Come on, come on.* Sweat stung his eyes as he shoveled.

The blaze became a bonfire.

"Trail the upper side!" he yelled, and nobody hacked at the fire line more furiously than he, for this Crossett-Western contract had been their little outfit's big break, the one they'd hoped might mean enough work to ride out the Depression.

Raw-throated, he shouted directions to the crew against the fire's gathering roar. Under his breath he cursed the flames, cursed the so-and-so who was late with the official shutdown order. Cursed himself too. He'd worked the woods since he was fourteen. Didn't need some fancy forester toy to know dynamite weather, and hadn't he had a gut hunch they ought to be shutting down?

The fire crackled through tinder-dry needles, spreading low along the ground. A hopeless fuel box, a cutover like this. Sparks were popping out, igniting splinters right and left. Six guys just couldn't cover it.

"Keep it away from those engines!" They'd scraped pennies for every haywire chunk of equipment they owned. If they lost it all now . . .

Squinting through smoke toward the draw, he saw help coming, thank God. Alarm must have sounded down at the mill. At the railroad tracks, men were jumping off a couple of gas-powered speeder cars, huffing up the steep slope with their tools. Looked like forty or so. That was more like it. Maybe they'd whip this thing yet.

The men threw themselves at the fire, each knowing now was the time to fight, now when a crew had a chance. If the fire got away, there'd be plenty of time later to sit on their butts and hash over the what-ifs. No, if they were ever going to stop it by the power of sweat and blood, shovels and axes, they had to give their best to stop it now.

The crew train whistle echoed down the old grade before Storie and Johnny reached home, and as they passed the bunkhouses at the edge of Blue Star, the clomp of calked boots and the raised voices inside told them that the hundred and fifty loggers employed by Sweetwater were already back in camp. Logging was done for the day.

"Don't surprise me they got shut down," Storie said. "This is sure the hottest, driest old wind's been blowin' through here. And from the east. That ain't the regular."

"Huh," Johnny said. "Hey, did you see me

right out there on the middle of that trestle? Boy howdy, I was really movin'!"

Look at him, puffed up proud as Mrs. Staver's rooster, already forgetting he'd fallen.

"Wadn't even that scary," he said.

"Oh, save your braggin' for Mama."

The air went out of him. "Now come on, Storie—" Suddenly he went sly. "Tell on me about the trestle and I'll tell you walked by the bunk-houses."

She shot him a dirty look. Daddy'd been after her to stay clear of the single men's quarters. No-body said, but she figured it had something to do with her suddenly coming up with what Mama called bosoms.

"Won't have no daughter a mine acting like some Earlene Bunch," Daddy said, and somehow Storie understood that he wasn't talking about running trestles or dynamiting the creek. No, it had to do with this other. He wouldn't take her on his knee anymore, and the way he looked at her, she felt like she'd already done something wrong, just to go and grow.

Well, jumpin' devils, could she help it? And didn't she wear baggy shirts and overalls to hide the whole business as best she could?

"Hey, know what Billy says?" Johnny whis-pered. "Says he'd like to kiss you."

"Oh yeah? Well, you can tell him for me it'll be a cold day in you-know-where before that ever happens!"

Johnny grinned to see he'd made her face go red. "I'm gonna see if Jake's in the shop," he said, heading off toward the big buildings where the thump of the mighty steam hammer was punctuated by the ring of those held by hand.

Billy Staver kissing her. She shuddered.

Picking her way home along the tracks, she matched each step with the varying widths between the ties. Log train tracks were laid in a hurry, nothing fancy. They were meant to last just long enough to get the timber out.

She passed the filing shack, the hog pen, the cookhouse and then the one-room school, set on the up side of the slope, still shut for the summer.

Miss Fowler was going to be their teacher again this year, and Storie looked forward to helping get things ready when she came up from Portland in two weeks. Not that Storie favored pushing a scrub brush in general, but oiling down the school's wood floors and cleaning off the dozen or so bolted-down desks was different. Last summer she and Miss Fowler had treated each book cover to a Lysol sponging and two coats of shellac to make them last longer. Now every time Storie smelled Lysol, she thought of that lovely time with her teacher, who was not all that much older than Storie herself and had the nicest way of telling about places she'd been, books she'd read.

For Storie it was like getting a peek at the big outside world without actually having to go down into it, something she wasn't at all eager to do.

This was her home; this was the place where she felt right. But she'd be in eighth grade this year and that was as far as Blue Star's school went. She had an idea Mama wanted her to go to Union High down in Forest Grove, which she hated to even think about. What a fish out of water she'd be there!

Past the commissary to the far end of the camp, she finally reached the fourteen family houses lining the tracks. The shingled cabins were built on skids so that they could be hauled on flatcars to the next campsite as soon as the men finished logging this section. After two years here, though, the brush had grown around the skids, and the cabins looked permanent enough with their flour sack curtains and tacked-on porches.

At the moment, each yard was dominated by a big log, delivered last week by the Sweetwater Timber Company's locomotive engine. Over the coming weeks, the logs would be reduced to stovewood lengths and stacked in the back woodsheds against the long, wet winter.

At Storie's place, the little garden Mama had grubbed out around the stumps looked pitiful in the heat, the clumps of sweet pea drooping down, near dead, the greens wilty too. Not that their gardens were ever much to brag on. "Dirt up here's good for growing one thing and one thing only," Daddy was always saying. "Trees."

But Mama was determined to put greens on

his plate whether he liked it or not. If she couldn't coax anything from the garden, she hunted watercress down by the creek, even though Daddy counted the sight of this on his plate as the ultimate insult. "Woman!" he'd bellow. "What are you thinking? Don't you dare be trying to feed me these leaves and grasses!"

Now Storie crossed the plank that spanned the drainage ditch between the tracks and the front porch steps.

"Hey there, Patches," she said to her calico cat, who slinked out from behind the sawed-off powder keg Mama'd made into a planter for her red geraniums. "Bet you'd like to take off that pretty fur coat on a day like this, huh?"

It was so blamed hot. Not a good day for baking up a berry pie in the wood-fired cookstove. But Mama'd have it going on any account. Daddy had to have his hot meals.

In the house, Storie set her bucket on the drainboard and went on through. On the back porch, Mama was pouring water for Daddy's wash. Her brown bobbed hair fell forward, leaving the back of her slender neck exposed above the crisscrossed straps of the apron she wore over her faded housedress. She was small, but strong. Had to be, to hoist heavy kettles like that.

Daddy had his shirt off and was scrubbing his hairy chest. Cleaning up to Mama's satisfaction was a real project for him after logging even a short day. Mud in the winter and dust in the sum-mer.

"Hey, Daddy," Storie said. "How's she loggin'? Get shut down?"

"Yep. Things are just too dry."

Storie loved the smell of fresh-cut fir he car-ried on him, the woodsy perfume of pitch.

"Well," she said, "too hot to work anyway."

"No work means no pay, little girl."

Storie and her mother glanced at each other. Daddy riding out the heat at home did not make for the pleasantest of afternoons. Mama said it wasn't really the money so much that worried him, he just couldn't stand idleness. A man had to be alert every minute in the woods if he hoped to end the day alive, so relaxing didn't come natural.

"I'm making a pie for you, Daddy."

"Well, now." He grinned. "That'd go good."

Storie smiled back, forgetting the heat. Maybe Mama was right about the importance of being a good cook. It felt nice to have the power to do something so simple that could perk up a grouchy man like that.

She went up to the edge of the woods to check on Snowflake, the orphan fawn she'd been nurs-ing.

Somebody must have shot the fawn's mother last spring, Storie figured. Folks up here paid no attention whatsoever to hunting seasons. Now, in August, Snowflake was starting to lose her white spots. Storie had been bottle-feeding her canned milk, but finally the delicate little animal was weaned. She bleated as Storie's familiar hand reached into the pen to pet her.

"You hungry, baby?" Storie talked to her pets a fair amount, but mostly under her breath. She didn't need people making fun of her. She gathered a few handfuls of grass at the woods' edge and put them in the pen. " 'Fraid your greens ain't one bit juicy today." She filled the water bucket from the outside pipe.

Sitting in the dust, she watched the fawn nibbling away. Deer were the loveliest creatures, she thought, the way they bounded through the forest. If you surprised a doe grazing, she would look up, flick her ears, then hold still as a statue. You could stare into those eyes for the longest time, trying to know and understand everything *she* knew from running wild and free in the woods.

"Someday you'll be out there in the forest again," Storie whispered, "soon as I get you growed up big enough." The cage was for Snowflake's protection from bigger animals more than anything else, for she would have followed Storie around like a house pet, given the chance. Storie was afraid to let her do that. How could the fawn go back to the wild if she got the idea she was a dog or a cat?

On the back porch, Mama handed Daddy his clean shirt.

"I'll get going on that there firewood," he said.

"Oh, now, honey, you don't have to work in this heat."

"Gotta get 'er done," Daddy said, taking up his crosscut saw. That was the first step. Then he'd use a sledgehammer and wedges and, finally, an ax.

Storie jumped up. "Help you, Daddy?"

"Naw, you don't have to."

"Oh, come on. You know it's easier with somebody on the other end." She grinned. "Says right there in the Bible, 'Two are better than one, for they have a good reward for their labor.' "

"It says that?" He winked. "I'll be darned."

Storie pushed and pulled, her hands gripping the smooth wooden handle, the rhythmic rasp of the saw filling the air.

So hard, she thought, on a day like this, to remember the wetness of winter—those damp two-blanket nights when the rain beat on the tar paper roof. You had to be able to imagine the sky pouring, though. You had to saw and chop and stack that wood. Otherwise, come December, you'd be trying to warm yourself with nothing but the memory of a hot August afternoon.

To the young lookout on South Saddle Mountain, the undulating ridges of surrounding
green forest seemed like an endless sea, and the
tower's swaying deck was his ship, riding the
waves.

Never had he scanned the panorama more in-
tently, for with a temperature of ninety-five degrees and humidity an appalling twenty-two per-
cent, he knew a spark could become a holocaust in
no time. And as a warden from the Tillamook Forest Protection Association had pointed out to him
the other day, with one lone Model T Ford pump

truck in its fire fighting arsenal, they had sure better catch early anything that might start up.

No one disputed that this was a forest worthy of protection: trees grown of the centuries, giants straight and strong that had burst as seedlings from the mountainsides and ravines and thrust themselves hundreds of feet into the sky long before the first white man set foot in the Northwest, thousands upon thousands of acres of the finest Douglas fir, hemlock and spruce on earth.

The beauty of this living green treasure had become familiar to the lookout after so many weeks at his post. He searched now for the unfamiliar, the telltale column of smoke. This he must do methodically, continuously, reminding himself to be glad of the tedium, considering the alternative.

Sometimes, during the long hours of watching for fire, he *thought* about fire. Looking over the vast wilderness, he imagined what it would have been like trying to survive out there in prehistoric times. In the depths of a wet, cold winter, longing for heat and light, how those first humans must have treasured the secret knowledge that a stick, rapidly twirled in a notch, could spark a pinch of waiting wood dust to flame.

And the power of that spark! It amazed the ranger when he pondered it. For a flood can't be triggered by one drop of water—but one spark of fire? Well, just watch what happens if you let two logs drag against each other in a forest, let a hot flicker fly into the tinder-dry duff . . .

Shortly after one o'clock on that long-to-be-remembered August afternoon, he grabbed his binoculars, alarm tingling down his spine. A thin plume of white smoke some six, seven miles to the northeast. He sighted along his firefinder, noting the section, township and range of the smoke, and hurried to phone the warden in Forest Grove.

Fire in Gales Creek.

Storie rolled out the pie crust oh so carefully.
You wanted to get it right the first time, Mama
always said. You couldn't be forever wadding it up
and starting over and expect it to come out nice
and flaky.

Although Storie found most cooking tiresome,
pie making pleased her somehow, maybe because
it was a once-in-a-while endeavor as opposed to
the disheartening business of continually produc-
ing all that everyday food—the beans and flapjacks and potatoes and other gut-filling grub you

had to keep piling up for a man. She had often seen her mother work hours to make a meal her father devoured in minutes. And sometimes by the time they had the dishes done, it was time to start right in on the next.

But a blackberry pie—that was like the hot, sweet taste of summer itself, baked with cloves in a golden crust.

"I suppose I ought to try making a pie for Harly," Alice Harlan from next door said, leaning in their doorjamb. "Probably wouldn't turn out, though. And I hate berry picking. All them stickers makes such a mess of your hands."

"Pretty soon your little Davey'll be big enough to do your picking," Mama said without looking up from the table where she was sketching a dress pattern on newspaper. "Then you'll be set."

Alice smiled vaguely. They all knew perfectly well, no matter how many bucketloads of berries were delivered to her, she wasn't about to make a pie. Alice simply refused to be shamed into joining the camp's frantic cooking and canning competition, a stand that Storie secretly admired. Even watching her own Harly putting away somebody else's pies with obvious relish didn't seem to bother Alice. "What do I care?" she'd say and add with a wink, "Long as her pies is all he's after!"

Now she came in and began drifting around the Rendalls' cabin. "Say, how about gettin' up a bridge game?"

"I don't think so," Mama said.

"Oh, come on. We could set up outside. You could die in these cabins on a day like this."

"Sorry, Alice," Mama said. "We just have too many things to do."

Alice sighed and looked over Mama's shoulder. "So what is it you're plannin' to make there?"

"Dress for Storie. My mother sent up this nice piece of fabric for it." She undraped a length of blue cotton dotted with flowers.

"And you're making the pattern yourself? I'd be scared to go cuttin' up good material like that."

"Well, I've done it before. And Alice, they want fifteen cents for a printed pattern. I'm not about to pay good money for something I can do myself. See? I'm going to copy it right off the picture in this magazine."

"That's real clever. But you know, you could buy a lot of patterns—heck, the whole dress—for the cost of the canned milk I seen Storie pourin' down that pet deer of hers."

Storie and Mama glanced at each other.

"Guess we all have to choose how we spend our money," Mama said. Just last week Alice had gone all the way down to Portland and paid a dollar twenty-five to have her hair waved. Bragged on what a bargain it was too. Mama just couldn't get over it.

"If Storie's pets make her happy," Mama added, "I don't begrudge her the milk."

"Hmm," Alice said, squinting at Storie. "Well,

if you're getting a grown-up new dress, you ought to let me fix your hair to go with it. I don't have the stuff for a permanent wave, but I watched how they cut mine. Bet I could do yours and water-wave it."

"Um, thanks, but no thanks."

"Storie has her own ideas about her hair," Mama added dryly.

Two years back, Storie had undone her braids and spent a pleasant spring afternoon snipping and tossing long blond strands from the back porch, just for the fun of watching the birds snatch them up for nests. By the time Mama had come home from Brightrain and caught her she'd looked a fright, and Mama'd had to trim what was left into the new bob style. Much as Mama had fussed, though, Storie hadn't been sorry. It had been worth it, to spot her own golden threads wound through birds' nests around camp for months afterward. She hadn't held still for her mother's scissors since, and her hair now hung halfway down her back.

Alice peered out the four-paned window into the side yard.

"You're so lucky with Tom, Margie. Look at him, tying into that wood already. Harly'll put it off until it's pouring rain, then act all hangdog when I make him go out and at least chop up some stove wood so I can cook his supper."

It was true, Mama was the envy of all the other women at Blue Star for this: she never had to say one pleading word to Daddy about fuel wood. She could keep her cooking and washing fires going from now till forever and he'd have that wood chopped up ahead of her. "You cook, so I'll chop," he always said. "Won't have folks see no wife a mine out there swinging no ax."

"You're right, I can't complain on that score," Mama said now. "Have you got some extra dough there, Storie? Why don't you bake up a special little pie for Johnny? He'd like that."

Storie nodded. What if Mama knew they were fixing to reward a kid who'd risked his neck on the rotten old trestle? He'd grabbed his lunch and taken off so fast they'd never said a word about his scraped cheek. Just a wonder how they let him run wild, go anywhere he wanted. They never seemed to worry much, not like they'd taken to worrying about her. *Stay clear of the bunkhouses.* What awful thing was Daddy imagining? She might get an earful of some of the men's bad words?

"Say," Alice said, "how come you and Tom didn't come on down to the dance at Vinemaple Saturday night?"

Storie's rolling pin stopped. "Did we miss a dance, Mama?" She always enjoyed the wild, foot-stomping music of the fiddles and accordions, and many a Saturday night she'd fallen asleep to it, dozing in a pile of coats and other children in the corner of one grange hall or another.

Mama directed her answer to Alice, ignoring

Storie. "It gets a little more complicated when the kids aren't babies you can park in a basket anymore."

"What do you mean?" Alice said. "This one here's old enough to dance herself."

"A fella from over at Camp Six asked me last time," Storie said. "Ain't that right, Mama?"

Mama leveled a look at Alice. "Tom was not real pleased about that."

"Oh," Alice said. "I get it."

The two women eyed Storie knowingly, keeping between themselves whatever it was they understood.

"Well, anyway," Alice went on, "you missed a lot of fun. And did you hear Jack Bunch got his nose broke again?"

"He did? No, I haven't seen him." Mama slipped a measuring tape around Storie's waist. "Mavis either, now I think of it."

"She's probably hiding out with another black eye while he sleeps off the cougar juice. Drinkin' and fightin', that's all he lives for."

"Poor Mavis. Poor little Earlene."

"Earlene ain't so little anymore," Storie pointed out, but her mother was following her own train of thought.

"What a sorry excuse for a man. I'll tell you, Storie, any man ever hits you, you walk the first time it happens. Don't wait till there's a houseful of babies to worry about. Understand?"

Storie nodded, disconcerted as usual by her mother's issuing instructions for grown-up life like it was all about to begin tomorrow.

Addressing Alice again, Mama lowered her voice. "They say Jack's been brewing beer in that little shanty out back of their place. Mr. Wicks catches him, he could lose his job. This is supposed to be a family camp."

"Oh, come on, Margie. Everybody wants a nip now and then. Nobody minds the law."

"I'm not talking about Prohibition. I'm talking about breaking Sweetwater's rules. He's lucky he's got a job. Pure foolishness to risk getting sent down."

As Storie pinched the dough into a fluted edging around Johnny's little pie pan, she heard voices outside. The men were gathering, as usual, at Daddy's chopping block.

"Now wouldn't you think they'd get their fill of loggin' while they're doin' it?" Alice said, watching out the window. "Oh no, if they ain't doin' it, they gotta be talkin' about it."

When Storie had the pies in the oven, she went out back to see if maybe it was the tiniest bit cooler there. She checked on Patches, who was stretched out in the shade, then climbed up to the top of the backyard stump and sprawled across it on her belly.

She could hear the men in the side yard. Alice was right, they never did tire of logging talk. They would rehash the day's work and speculate on tomorrow's. They analyzed how a side ought to be laid out and how many loads of logs they'd likely get from the section of timber they'd be working next.

Storie had never realized how much their woods words were like a foreign language until Grandma came up to visit one time and Storie found herself explaining that no, Daddy's rain gear wasn't really made of tin, they just called them tin pants. Or that the crummy was the train car that carried the men to work in the woods. When Grandma demanded to know why any self-respecting man would allow his logging outfit to be called a gyppo operation, Daddy'd said, "Oh, Maude, it don't mean nothin' bad anymore. Just means a little old independent show, that's all."

Honestly, you could listen to these men fling their talk around for hours without understanding a word unless you were a logger. Or, Storie often thought proudly, the daughter of a logger.

This evening she let the drone of it flow past her and only perked up to listen when it suddenly stopped dead. What was going on?

Mr. Wicks, the camp superintendent, was marching down the tracks, aiming himself straight toward the group of men. Anybody could tell he was no logger. He had a softness about him that came from pushing a pen instead of a saw, and looked as if he'd been putting away the same prodigious meals as the rest of them without quite burning it all off.

"Boys," he greeted them, nodding. "Don't have to tell you we got tinderbox conditions up here. We'll be sticking to hoot-owl shift, and I want everybody on alert, extra careful."

A low murmur of assent ran through the group.

"Just got word—fire going over at Gales Creek."

"That so?" Storie's father looked over his shoulder to the southeast.

Mr. Wicks nodded. "Some little family show. What I hear, they'll get her licked. Still, let's take it as a warning."

The men shifted uneasily, a couple of them hooking thumbs in their red suspenders and craning back to scowl at the sky.

Storie sat up cross-legged and sniffed the air. Was that smoke she smelled? And just how far away was Gales Creek?

In darkness, Storie woke and heard her mother rattling pans in the kitchen. No sign of dawn. Hoot-owl shift started early, the men heading out to get in what work they could before the heat and lack of humidity shut operations down. Storie lay in her bunk, stroking Patches' soft fur, breathing in the aroma of Daddy's breakfast: hotcakes, slabs of pork, eggs, blackberry pie and coffee.

"A logger's like a steam lokey engine," her mother always said. "Just burns up the fuel. Full-time job keeping one of them stoked."

And a woman had to watch out, she warned

Storie, for as much as she might sweat over a stove or a washtub, it was not the same as climbing a two-hundred-and-fifty-foot tree or dragging a misery whip through four-foot butts all day long. A wife who sat down and matched her man bite for bite would soon look like Mrs. Staver, big as a rain barrel.

Johnny rolled out of bed and pushed aside the curtain that served as a door between the main part of the little house and the lean-to addition they shared.

"Can I go up with you, Dad?"

"Not today, son."

"Aw, why not?" Johnny craved being part of the heat, dust and noise as the men and machines leveled the timber.

"Likely we'll get us shut down before we're even started, weather like this. You stick close to the swimmin' hole, Johnny. Tag along another day."

Used to be me who'd go along, Storie thought, remembering how the men would call her Little Logger and tweak her braids. They could never seem to get over her eyes, which were a strange and lovely amber. "Why, Tom," they'd say, "this little gal of yours has cougar eyes, sure enough."

She'd always enjoyed their fond teasing, but hearing Johnny beg to go, she realized she'd never loved the logging itself the way he did. Watching the tree-topper work his way up that first spar tree had always scared her, even though that was the part Daddy expected her to like the most. After all, it was the closest thing in a logging operation to a death-defying circus act. Everybody knew if the man's ax slipped and nicked his sling, that was it.

"Your grampa, Papa Pete, fell off a spar tree he was riggin'," Daddy had told her. "Dove head-first into a nest of cuttings. Darned if he didn't climb out and go right back up the tree to finish the job."

"Golly."

"And that, peewee, is a story known in every camp from Coos Bay to Aberdeen, 'cause a straight fall of two, three hundred feet—well, most times a man's soul has gone to hell before his body even hits the ground."

"He was sure lucky."

"Oh, I don't know about that. I'd say it just shows what every logger knows—a man don't go till it's his time, and that's all there is to it."

Well, even if that was the case, Storie had decided she got no thrill from being there to see for herself if somebody's time had come or not.

And another thing about the logging—she worried about the animals, the chipmunks that came around to share lunch, the birds and deer. Must scare the living daylights out of them when the shout of *Timmmmmberrrrr!* rolled out and one of those forest giants came thundering down in a cloud of dust and bouncing branches, shaking the earth itself.

Once she asked her father what happened to the animals when all the trees were logged off. "Heck, honey," he said, "they just run off to the next bit of woods, that's all..Truth is, they love a clear-cut. Lets in the light." But when she pressed him why they couldn't leave a tree standing here and there for the birds and animals, he said she asked too many questions.

Johnny's questions never bothered Daddy, though, because what Johnny wanted was every last detail about the raucous, fire-breathing machines, details their father seemed more than happy to supply. No wonder he was more likely to invite Johnny instead of her to go along these days.

After Johnny burrowed back into bed, Storie swung her legs out. " 'Scuse me there, Patches." The linoleum felt cool and gritty under her bare feet.

"You gettin' up?" Johnny whispered.

"Just goin' to make a visit." She tried for a bit more delicacy now that she wasn't exactly a little girl anymore.

He rolled over. "Watch out for cougars."

He was only half joking, she knew. Unlike her, he avoided dark-of-the-night outhouse runs. He wouldn't admit it, but the animals scared him.

Sure, Storie's neck hair would rise at the half-human scream of a cougar same as anyone's, and she didn't know what she'd do if she met with a bear on a trail like Grandma Rendall did one time.

But she wouldn't startle if a bitty little mouse ran over her foot, or scamper back to the house if a raccoon snorted at her from behind the woodpile.

Slipping through the main room, she mumbled a good morning to her parents and pushed open the back door.

The air smelled smoky, but that wasn't unusual. Something was always burning this time of year—logging slash deliberately torched, or the stump piles of ranchers who were trying to carve and burn farms out of the forest. But now the smell reminded her of the new forest fire.

"Daddy? How far'd you say Gales Creek is?"

"Oh, a good ten miles."

"Think this smoke's from there?"

"Naw. Wind ain't even blowing this way."

Out on the well-worn path she stopped and let her head fall back. The sky glittered in the swath between the treetops. She loved being out at night or just before dawn. The world showed you something different then, an unaccustomed quiet, or maybe the moon, hanging in the west, where you didn't see it so often.

Tonight a hooty owl called out soft and low and she wondered, as she always did when she heard one, if it could be her own baby owl, come back to visit.

The spring before, she'd come upon a young horned owl out in the woods a mile or so up the creek trail, two gleaming yellow eyes nestled in a ball of feathers and fluff, almost as big as an adult but too young to fly. Must have fallen from its nest, Storie thought, squinting up into the tree branches. Wasn't going to come to any happy end here on the forest floor, that much was sure.

So she gathered it up and carried it home.

"Well, stars and garters," Mama said. "How do you plan to feed it? Owls hunt mice."

"We got traps," Storie said. "I can hunt mice too."

As it turned out, she didn't have to. That evening she was sitting out back, admiring her latest charge in the coop she'd built of chicken wire scraps begged off of Mrs. Staver.

At the rustling of wings, Storie looked up and saw the dark shape of an owl in flight. Something dangled from its talons. She held her breath as the mother owl descended, alighting on the cage top. As Storie watched in wonder, the owl pushed some small rodent through the screening.

How had the mother found her owl child? The nest was at least a mile away.

Every evening Storie waited and watched this faithful ritual, and the mother owl never failed to appear with dinner. The baby owl grew quickly. Finally one evening Storie opened the cage, and the young owl followed her mother off into the treetops.

Storie never named that owl. A silly pet name just didn't seem right for such a dignified creature, and besides, she'd never felt for one moment like she owned it. No, it had been her privilege just to watch this pair. Now, whenever she heard the who-whoing of the owls, she liked to think it was them, letting her know they were near.

On her way back to the house, she stopped by Snowflake's pen. All quiet. Quiet in the trees too. Even the birds still slept.

Then she heard the front door open and the tap of the spikes on Daddy's calked boots across the ditch plank.

Rex Staver greeted him. "Hear your boy Johnny ran that old trestle yesterday."

Whoa! Storie tensed. Johnny was going to catch it after all.

"Did he?" Surprisingly, Daddy sounded halfway tickled. "That little son of a gun. I've told him to stay clear a that thing."

"Yeah, I whipped Billy when I heard about it. Never told how we done the same thing'n we was little britches."

"I'll get after Johnny. His mother'd faint dead away, she hears this. But I tell ya, Rex, he'll make a heck of a logger someday."

"Billy too, he don't get kilt first!"

Storie stood in the shadows, listening to the gruff greetings of the men gathering up where the crew train's engine cut a yellow swath through the blackness. One by one the kerosene lamps in the little wooden cabins went out.

The human steam lokey from each cabin had been stoked; the women were going back to bed.

"Storie Faye?" Mama said. "Run this meat order on up to the commissary for me. When
you get back we'll see about cutting out your
dress."

Storie scraped leftovers into a dish for
Patches. "Mama, you don't have to make me no
new dress."

"Don't say 'no new dress.' And don't you think
it'd be nice to have one for the first day of school?"

Storie shrugged and took the slip of paper
Mama handed her. Sometimes it seemed like
Mama wasn't picturing Storie's real school up the

tracks, but some big school with lots of girls where dresses mattered. Here, since Earlene had quit to work at the cookhouse, Storie was the only big girl, and she would just as soon have stuck to overalls.

"At any rate," Mama said, "I had in mind *you* making this one. Time you learned to sew."

Storie edged out the door. With a little luck, Mama might get busy on something else and forget.

In the dusty yard next door, Alice's little Davey was using some beat-up toy train cars to haul stick logs on the track he'd scraped around the tree trunks.

"That's some loggin' show you got yourself," Storie said. An upright stick rigged with string served as the spar pole, and a spool of thread represented the drum and cable of the steam donkey engine. "You do that all yourself?"

He nodded. "I seen how when Mama hiked me up to the show."

"Say, where'd you get them sewing machine bobbins?"

"What? These little round metal dealies? These is my drums and blocks, not no sewin' machine parts."

"They were before you swiped 'em."

"I never! I found 'em!"

"Okay, now, don't throw a whingding. Anyway, your riggin's pretty slick."

He was a lot smarter than you'd think to watch him in school, Storie decided. He'd started last year and still hadn't picked up one word of reading. Mama thought it was just a shame how his mother didn't seem to care.

"What's he need readin' for?" Alice would say. "Heart's set on being a logger like his daddy. And his daddy don't read."

Mama always had to bite her tongue, Storie could tell, when Alice would go off the very next minute with her wishful talk about how she hated moving from one log camp shack to the next, and what-all fun things there were for folks living down in town.

"She just doesn't see it," Mama would say to Storie later, "how a little reading and schooling gives a person more choices."

Johnny was set on logging too, and could hardly wait for his first pair of calked boots. He figured he only had about five years to go until he could sign on for the starting woods job, whistle punk, the boy who passes the signal from the choker setter to the donkey engineer that a log's hooked up and ready to be yarded in.

Mama tried to point out to him there were other good, higher-paying woods jobs for a man with some education—civil engineer or machinist. Even Daddy himself sometimes said, "Oh, you don't want to be a logger, son. I'm only a logger 'cause that's all I can be."

Storie doubted Daddy believed this in his heart, though. What he did took plenty of education—just not the schoolbook kind. Why, except for those high-pay jobs Mama talked about, he knew every logging job there was—falling, bucking, setting the chokers. He'd put in his seasons of balancing six feet up on a springboard wedged into the butt of some giant, he and a pal dragging their saw back and forth the better part of a day to fell the one tree. He'd buckled on climbing spurs and done his share of rigging back when he was younger too. These days the other men looked to him to lay out the side and choose a spar tree with a good flat landing for gathering the logs. Everyone wanted to be on Big Tom's crew and he knew it.

So Storie didn't quite buy it when he claimed to be nothing but an uneducated old logger. Besides, if he really felt that low about it, why was he so quick to sneer at farmers, ministers, or any person in pants who sat behind a desk or stood before a classroom?

In the end, Johnny got the message: logging was the only fit occupation for a real man.

"But nobody's saying a man can't read books and still log the woods," Mama kept reminding him. She took pride in their meager library arranged in an old wooden saw box she'd nailed to the wall—the Bible, Storie's well-worn bird book, Mama's own childhood favorites. She sent regularly to the State Library in Salem for books too, and those were kept separate at one end. She wanted to be faithful about sending them back on time.

So far, Johnny never read anything but the

funny papers. Little Davey here, playing in his dusty yard, looked like he was headed in the same direction.

"Storie Faye!" Mama stuck her head out the door. "Get to the store *now*! They want the meat orders first thing."

"I'm going," Storie said, heading up the tracks. Mama was always sending her to the store to avoid going herself. She called the commissary the robbisary, because of Mr. Clinkinbeard's only-store-around high prices. Also, he was a grouch who made no secret of his disdain for all the "she-stuff" in camp. Log camps had been better, he claimed, before men started moving in their wives.

So what was it he didn't like? Storie always wondered. The pots of flowers on the porches? The Christmas pageant in the cookhouse? The sound of Miss Fowler playing the schoolhouse piano and singing, the lovely, heartbreaking words drifting out into a late-summer evening?

In the gloaming, oh my darling
When the lights are growing dim
Will you think of me and love me
As you did so long ago?

Maybe he had some long-lost love, Storie thought, and didn't want to be reminded.

As she passed the LaBranche house, May came out on the porch with a broom.

"Morning, Mrs. LaBranche."

"Oh, Storie." She pushed back her soft brown fluff of hair and smiled her sweet smile. "Much as I'm enjoying being a Mrs. now, you know you can call me May." She had the gentlest way about her. She was, as Daddy put it, skinny as a sack of deer horns, except for the huge bulge of her belly—her first baby near ready to be born.

"Looks like another hot one," she said.

" 'Fraid so."

From down by the creek, Storie heard the boys' shouts. That was the place to be on a day like this. Maybe she could go if she ever got done with all the chores Mama had lined up.

"So tell me, Storie Faye, does it always get this hot up here?" May's husband, Charlie, had just been hired on by Sweetwater, so they were new in camp.

"No, this is real unusual."

"Good!"

"Fact, I can't remember it ever being so hot."

May braced her hands against the small of her back and sighed. "Feels like the whole camp is sitting smack in the middle of a big bake oven."

Good way to put it. Storie walked on. If only the west wind would return, carrying the cool dampness of the ocean. Since the east wind started up, walking on the forest floor had become like treading on crushed cornflakes, and Mama kept saying her skin felt so dry she was like one of those dolls with shriveled apples for heads.

Storie opened the slip of paper in her fist.

Mama could have just told her the meat order, but she seemed to think it was nicer to put it down in her pretty writing. Lamb chops. Boy howdy, even on a day like this? Maybe someday, Storie thought, I'll live down in the valley, and on hot days I'll eat nothing but ice cream right out of my own refrigerator.

At the store, she checked the thermometer nailed up outside. Eighty-four degrees at only nine in the morning!

It wasn't much cooler inside the dimly lighted commissary. Storie stood a moment, letting her eyes adjust. Alice Harlan was leafing through one of the magazines. She liked listening to the radio up here, she always said. Made her feel closer to the outside world.

"Awk! Pretty girl! Pretty girl!"

Storie blushed, even if it was just Jack, Mr. Clinkinbeard's crested mynah. He was a handsome bird, black with white wing patches and a yellow bill. She'd like him a whole lot better if he'd learn to say something less embarrassing, though.

She sidled over to the cage. "How's she loggin', Jack?" she whispered. "Can you say that? How's she loggin'?"

"Likes pretty girls better'n he likes loggers," Alice said without emerging from her magazine. "Oh, look here." She held a fashion illustration under Storie's nose. "Now wouldn't you just *love* one of these big fur collars they're showing for fall?"

Storie regarded the picture with what interest she could muster. "Well . . . little hot for even thinkin' about fur, ain't it?"

Alice laughed. "When I'm picturing myself in this, I'm so far away in my mind, the weather here at Blue Star really don't matter. In my dreams I'm in . . . San Francisco, that's it! In the cool fog."

"Sounds pretty good," Storie agreed. "Still, I kinda favor live animals over dead ones."

"Oh, kid." Alice shook her head. "You're a funny one."

Storie tried to stretch out her look around the small store as long as possible, but there wasn't a whole lot to see. Mr. Clinkinbeard didn't bother arranging the merchandise with the idea of tempting anybody. The stock of woolen mackinaws, boots and long underwear sat in dusty boxes on the shelves. A man either needed these items or he didn't. He wasn't going to buy a hickory shirt just because it looked good on some mannequin like you'd see down in Forest Grove.

Same thing for food—no display. Mr. Clinkinbeard expected you to walk in knowing what you wanted from the storeroom.

"Somethin' I can help you with, sis?" he said.

Storie gave him the meat order.

"Come on back for it towards supper," he said, "and we'll have it cut for you."

She lingered a long moment over the box of candy bars and chewing gum, debating which she'd buy next time she lucked on to a nickel. Then she stepped out into the glare.

At the dining hall she stuck her head in for a breath of the wonderful smell of baking bread wafting from the kitchen.

Earlene was just finishing sweeping. She nodded sullenly at Storie before disappearing inside.

They had never gotten along, even though Mama'd had high hopes when Earlene's father had been hired by Sweetwater three years earlier. "A girl just two years older than you, won't that be nice? A little girlfriend so you won't always have to be running with the boys." But within minutes of their introduction Earlene was saying, "My mama can lick your mama," and Storie was replying, "My mama don't fight," and that was the end of that.

Another camp waitress appeared and started setting the long tables for the next meal, putting at each numbered place a heavy white china plate with a bowl and cup turned upside down on it.

"Hi, Wanda," Storie said.

Wanda scowled. She had black bobbed hair that wouldn't hold a finger wave. She'd told Storie once she was part Indian.

"What's the matter?"

"Hoot-owl shift, that's what. Men showing up at any old hour, looking for food. Wears us out. Don't rain soon, Bridey and I are gonna drop dead."

*   *   *

NOTHING LEFT TO do but go home and face her sewing lesson. Storie started back along the tracks. Davey was still at his game.

"We're done loggin' this show," he called across the ditch as she drew alongside. "Time to torch the slash!"

Wait. Was that a match? He struck it.

"Davey, no! Blow it out this instant!" She scrambled down the rail grade.

Startled, he blew. The flame faded, then flared.

They both started blowing. To their horror, it sprang back every time.

"It's burnin' me!" Davey cried, and dropped it.

Storie pounced, stamping the dry needles. "Get a bucket!" She kicked at the smoldering duff until Davey huffed back with a sloshing pail to douse it.

They stared at the puddle.

When her heart had stopped thumping quite so hard, Storie turned on him. "Davey Harlan. Don't you never play with matches! You hear? Don't you know this whole place is ready to catch on fire almost all by itself?"

"I tried to blow it out," Davey said. "Why wouldn't it?"

Storie frowned, wondering the same thing herself. "You better go up and fetch your mama home from the store. The camp ain't safe with you on your own."

After he'd shuffled off, hanging his head,

Storie picked up his abandoned box of matches. She glanced over her shoulder. Mrs. Potter was pinning up diapers several houses down but wasn't looking this way. Carefully Storie struck a match. When the flame flared, she blew. For an instant it seemed it would die; then, as she watched in fascination, it blazed back to life. She blew again. Same thing. Just before it burned her fingers, she dropped it onto the wet spot where they'd emptied the bucket.

She ground it in and scanned the bleached-out sky. She'd seen the train engineer studying a sky like this once. A fire-in-the-sky day, he called it.

She looked down at her feet. The wind had already dried up the puddle's last traces.

"Oh, there's that darn whistle." Mama began clearing the sewing things off the table. One long blast, one short meant logging shut down for the day. "We've got to get your daddy's lunch on."

Storie laid the pile of cut-out fabric pieces on a cot in the main room. "Didn't you already pack him a bucket?"

"He probably ate that hours ago. Besides, a man isn't going to sit down at his own table and open a lunch box. He'll expect a real meal."

Storie looked around, wondering where this meal was going to come from.

"Weather like this," Mama said, "I should know they'll be home early, but I keep thinking a little fog'll roll in." She hustled back and forth, pulling down jars of preserves, a loaf of bread, whatever she could find.

"Now, Storie Faye," she went on, "you have the most important job. You get that table set. A man comes home and finds the table laid, he figures food's on the way. He won't even notice if it's another half hour before he's eating. But if he walks in and no dishes are out, well, it won't matter if it's all on the stove ready to dish up, he gets downhearted." She stopped. "Now what else can I give him?"

"The rest of my blackberry pie," Storie offered, laying the silverware on the oilcloth-covered table.

"No, that's long gone. Finished it off at breakfast. Remarked how good it was too." She flashed Storie a smile. "Said you were getting to be quite the cook."

Storie flushed with pleasure.

When the house shook with the passing of the shay, Storie went out to meet her father. Tightrope walking along one rail, she watched as the men got off the train up by the offices. The single men, a hundred or more, headed on toward the bunkhouses, but her father and the other family men turned and came swinging their lunch buckets back down the track.

Storie couldn't help admiring her father as the best of the bunch. It wasn't that he was bigger or stronger. Mr. Staver was actually taller, and all the men were well muscled or they wouldn't last one morning in the woods.

But somehow her father seemed made of finer stuff. He was handsome and carried himself like a king in his hacked-off pants and red felt hat. Even tired and covered with dust, he held his chin up, walking those tracks like a man who feels he's in the very spot on this earth he's supposed to be. The men beside him would glance his way as they talked, like they were hoping he agreed with whatever they said, wanting him to laugh at their jokes.

He, however, kept his eyes focused ahead, reminding her of some tall, straight forest giant, solid and true-grained.

"Hey, Daddy," she said as they approached, intending to add their usual greeting but suddenly feeling shy in front of the other men. Instead she waited until they were on their own back porch. "How's she loggin', Daddy?"

"Well, I'll tell you," he answered, "if you don't repeat it to your mother. It's hotter'n hollerin' hell out there!"

"Daddy!" But she was laughing.

Amazingly, by the time he got washed up, Storie's mother had a passable spread on the table and a clean apron on herself. She'd rounded up Johnny so that the three of them could eat token bites while Daddy put away his meal.

"So how's it going up there, Tom?" Mama said,

passing him a plate of pickles. She believed meal-times should include pleasant conversation, and knew logging was just about the only topic Daddy would discuss with any enthusiasm.

"Head push ain't too happy with that back corner of soft fir we're in," he said. "Awful lot of rot in that old stuff. Shoulda been cut years ago."

Mama nodded encouragingly, as if hoping for more, but Daddy was busy forking up beans. Loggers have a hard time talking and eating at the same time, Mama always told Storie. It must start out in their bachelor days.

You could sure see that in the dining hall. Once in a while Daddy would take them up there to give Mama a meal off. Those men could put away huge dinners in ten minutes flat with nothing but the sounds of chewing, the clanking of the heavy china, and grunts of "Pass this" and "How 'bout some of that?"

"Ain't talkin' allowed?" Storie whispered to her father once, edging closer to him on the dining hall bench. He laughed and later said the custom actually might have been a rule once, probably started back when times were rougher and two loggers could hardly trade six words without they'd start punching each other. Either that or the cook was determined nobody'd get a chance to bellyache out loud about the grub.

So Mama served up leading questions along with her food, determined to get Storie's father and brother used to the idea of commenting on things a bit between bites.

"And what have you been up to this morning?" she asked Johnny now.

"Oh, nothing." He stuffed peanut-buttered bread in his mouth.

"You must have been doing *something*. Where were you? Down by the crick?"

"We wash schwimmun and Sam wannada—"

"Oh, please, not with your mouth full!"

"Y'see, Margie," Daddy said. "Eating and talking just don't mix."

Mama narrowed her eyes. "People manage it," she said. "Polite people."

Daddy smirked.

"Well," she said, trying to ignore this, "what do you hear about the Gales Creek fire? Up at the store they're saying it might be under control by tonight."

He nodded. "Got some of them CCC boys on it."

"What's a CCC boy?" Storie asked.

"Civilian Conservation Corps," Mama said. "Part of the president's new plan. You know, to help get us out of these bad times."

Bad times. Storie knew they were in them because folks said so constantly, but just looking around Blue Star Camp, she couldn't see it. Things seemed pretty much the same as they always had.

"President Roosevelt's idea," Mama went on, "is to take young men who need jobs and put them to work in the woods."

Dad snorted. "And what the heck are a bunch of city kids gonna know about the woods? Nothing but babies, I hear. Skinny little runts."

"Now, Tom, that's unkind. They probably haven't been fed right. Don't you think they deserve a chance?"

"Heck, yes. Give 'em a chance. I hope they *do* get that fire out. Turns out Sweetwater's got some holdings over in that country, so if it gets outta hand, you can guess who's gonna be playing smoke-eater."

"Tom! You?"

"Me and everybody else here."

"Daddy?" Storie interrupted. "If the fire gets away from them, well, what happens to the animals?"

Her father shrugged. "They run away."

"Really?"

"Well, sure. What are you worried about? The deer? Now, honey, you know how fast they spring through the brush. Probably take off at the first whiff of smoke."

"So you've heard talk of sending you to the fire lines?" Mama said.

"That's right. 'Course, it's a paycheck either way, but I'd sure rather cut trees than fight fires."

"Unfortunately," Mama said, "there's probably a lot of men these days who'd be tickled to fight fires for a paycheck."

"That's right," Daddy said. "Wouldn't surprise me to see some on-purpose carelessness, if you know what I mean."

"Daddy!" Storie said. "You think somebody'd touch off a fire just to get himself a job fightin' it?"

"Been known to happen, honey."

"But—to burn up all them trees? Burn the animals right outta their homes?"

He put up his hands. "Hey, I ain't defending it, I just said—"

"Well, *I* say anybody'd do that is so low he . . . he . . . why, he ain't fit to oil the hinges of a skunk's stinker!"

"Storie!" Mama said. "I do wish you'd talk more ladylike."

"Well, I ain't no lady," Storie said.

"Nope." Daddy laughed, reaching out his big hand to tousle her hair. "You're my girl."

Tuesday, August 15, 3:00 p.m., Gales Creek

A boy with a soot-blackened face and a pair of government-issue boots stood panting in the newest Gales Creek firebreak. Scrape it down to mineral soil, they'd been told. Dirt that won't burn.

He was doing his best, but gosh, whoever expected this? Seemed like one day he was home in Missouri, worrying away the long idle hours, the next he was out West, blistering his hands fighting a sure enough forest fire. How he'd been craving some good, honest work! Well, now he had it. A dollar a day and no quitting. Tired? Need a break? Too bad. They had to stop this thing now.

A crew had a fighting chance against a ground fire, the fire bosses told them. As long as it burned in slash or tore through the undergrowth without running up the big trees, they might be able to trail around it, hack the fuel away in a swath wide enough to form a firebreak. So far, though, this fire had jumped every line their CCC troop had laid out. Now, after a day of burning in the cutover, it was headed for the ridge top and a vast stand of live, three-hundred-foot-tall trees, the ones he and the other Midwest boys just couldn't get over. Trees growing so tall and thick the sunlight hardly made it to the ground. Trees four of them couldn't grab hands around.

Would *this* line hold? Lordy, it *had* to. He glanced over his shoulder: thick green timber at his back, another couple of frantic kids on each side. Purely pitiful, he thought. Nothing but a handful of exhausted boys standing between that amazing forest and the fire that was starting to seem to him like some evil monster.

What happened to that fire boss, anyway? The one who promised it was his job to keep track of the escape routes if they had to run for it. Said the best way might be back through the fire itself. Could that be right?

The hot east wind was worse than ever. Burning embers were starting to blow over the break.

He jumped on one, beating it down. Meanwhile six more ignited around him. His chest seized. *"We can take it,"* he muttered, trying to encourage himself with their CCC motto. But panic surged through him. His face blazed with the heat, his eyes stung with smoke. *We can take it . . .* The ground itself seemed to burn, forcing him backward into the trees.

Like a fairy-tale dragon, the wind reared back and blasted a fiery breath at the trees. Coughing, he staggered, watching in horror as the flames crackled upward into the lower boughs. Oh God, it was going all the way up. He stopped, transfixed by the spectacle. It was doing that fearsome thing he'd overheard those loggers talking about this morning with such dread, such awe.

It was crowning.

Bright flames flashed skyward; in a deafening roar the trees exploded into giant torches, each igniting the next, in moments forming a canopy of fire above the men, an inferno that hurled sparks and firebrands far ahead to the west.

"That's it!" someone yelled. "Run! This way!"

Dropping his shovel, the boy tore after the others in a shower of red-hot embers.

Like everyone else in camp, Storie understood
the language of the steam donkey whistles,
the signals shrieked from ridge to ravine that told
in code the story of the day's logging progress.

Usually the whistles were no more than background noise, but seven long blasts and two short
—that was the combination to turn stomachs. The
dead whistle. Man down. Send a stretcher.

On Wednesday morning, in the houses along
the tracks, women unconsciously began counting
at the first screaming blast.

One . . . Storie tensed. The fire whistle?

That was long-short, repeated. Gales Creek was burning out of control, they said . . . Two . . . another long. *Not* the fire whistle. They kept up, long and mournful . . . six . . . and seven. Two short blasts, then silence.

Mama came in from her washing on the back porch. She and Storie looked at each other. Storie felt the dish she'd been drying start shaking in her hand. *Please, don't let it be Daddy.* She set it on the drainboard and followed her mother out front.

Mrs. Staver was already marching up the tracks. Johnny came hurrying from the creek path with Sam and Billy. Alice appeared on her porch, puffing a cigarette with her arms pressed tight to her sides. Storie and her mother clustered with the other women in a nervous knot at the X of the camp's two main tracks, watching the main office, waiting for clues.

"What's happening?" May LaBranche called from her porch.

They glanced at each other, silent. Finally Mrs. Staver went back. Somebody had to explain.

Watching, Storie could tell the exact instant May caught on, because her whole off-balance little body sagged, and Mrs. Staver had to prop her up. She helped the white-faced May down the steps and up the tracks toward the rest of the women and children. Nobody could go about their business when the man down whistle blew, even if their only business on this morning ought to be lying calm and easy on a cot.

Please, don't let it be Daddy, Storie kept praying, knowing everyone else was praying the same for whoever they had up on the show. For now, the misery was divided equally; in a few minutes one of them might be feeling a whole lot worse. Or maybe the injured worker was one of the young, single men from the bunkhouse. Oh, she hoped so . . . but what an awful thought. They had mothers too, didn't they? Sweethearts down in Brightrain and Forest Grove? Well, what about Jack Bunch? Maybe she could hope it was him? Then she glanced at his wife and daughter. They looked as wrought up as the rest of them.

She wondered again if it was true, about a man not going until it was his time. Oh Lord, so many ways for a man to die up there—crushed under a rolling log, struck by a mainline cable. Or a logger could have the plain bad luck to be standing under a branch torn loose in some past storm, a limb that had rested precariously until this fatal moment, now to fall, the warning crack of splintering wood masked by the staccato bark of the steam donkey engine.

An ominous quiet hung over the woods.

The women stepped off the tracks as the speeder car came rattling from the main camp area, heading up for the show. Storie thought Mr. Wicks's eyes met her mother's for just an instant. Did that mean something? But how could it? Right now, even he probably didn't know the identity of the fallen man.

Storie fixed her gaze on the faded daisy print fabric of her mother's apron pocket. Inside it, Mama's hand worried a couple of clothespins. Her other arm went out to gather Johnny close.

Storie thought of her father, working, sweating in the heat. Leaving the snug cabin on frigid mornings too, working in the cold to keep them fed. A vision of life without him rose before her. No big Tom Rendall, swaggering down the tracks at the end of the day in his red suspenders. Daddy, home from the big woods, covered in dust and smelling wonderfully of the sap of firs, his face lighting up when he sees her. "Hey, peewee, how's she loggin'?"

She stared up the tracks.

They watched Mr. Wicks's wife, Jeannette, make her way from her house down to the camp office. As she went in, the distant rumble of the machinery grinding back to work up on the show rolled over them like a small gift of grace. Storie took one easier breath.

"Nobody dead," Mrs. Staver explained to May LaBranche. "They'd shut down for the rest of the day if there was."

The women spared May by neglecting to point out that a call for the speeder still meant a serious injury. For a mere broken arm, a man would be expected to hike down the track on his own, like Daddy did that time back at White Star.

What if it's Daddy, Storie thought, and he's

hurt so bad he can't work anymore? How would they live, without any money at all? Probably they'd go down to Grandma's little farm on the outskirts of Forest Grove. Daddy would hate that, though. He could hardly stand three days of denning up during a snow. If he had to stay on a farm with Uncle Ralph, he'd go crazy.

He thought Mama's brother was a fool for going on the big march back to Washington, D.C., with the other war veterans, trying to collect their service bonuses early. "That prune picker wasted a whole year," Daddy would always say. "I coulda got him on up here."

But more than having to listen to Uncle Ralph's talk, Daddy'd hate not being able to work. Never put on his cork boots and ride the crummy out to the woods again? Why, that'd kill him right there. He'd probably rather have a log roll over him this instant and be done with it.

With the sounds of the steam donkey starting up again out in the log woods, the women knew the stretcher carriers had gone back to work and it wouldn't be long before the speeder rounded the curve by the freight platforms.

When it finally came clattering, they clutched their children's shoulders and watched it pull past and stop up by the office.

"Hank Hill," the superintendent said as the women approached.

"Thank God," whispered May LaBranche,

closing her eyes in relief. It wasn't her Charlie. Then she glanced around, guilty, her lip caught between her teeth.

But she'd only put to words what they'd all felt.

"Oh, honey, don't look," Mrs. Potter said, pulling her little Evie back from the open car.

Getting a glimpse of the man, Storie sucked in her breath. Good thing she'd already heard it wasn't her father. With so much blood, she might not have been able to tell. Actually, nobody recognized this young Hank Hill, bloodied or not. He must have been one of the new ones.

"Mama, Johnny's looking," Storie whispered.

"Good," Mama said under her breath. "I want him to remember this."

Jeannette Wicks came out of the camp office and climbed onto the speeder.

"We've phoned for the ambulance to meet us at Brightrain," she told her husband, settling on the wooden bench beside the injured boy.

When the speeder had taken off, May's faint voice was the first to break the silence. "Does this happen very often?"

"Oh, no!" Mrs. Staver said. "Why, I can't hardly remember the last time."

Storie glanced at her mother. Mrs. Staver must have a very short memory. Only last month they'd all run out here just this same way and waited, sick with fear, to learn that Ole Johansen had got his arm pinned between two logs.

"Let's get you back to your place," Mrs. Staver said to May.

Suddenly the women glanced around, shuddering as if awakened from a bad dream. The boys crept off to the creek. Storie became aware again of the terrible heat. She wanted to get back to the house, where at least they wouldn't be standing bareheaded in the blazing sun.

When they reached their own back porch, Storie said, "I hate it that we always have to worry Daddy'll get hurt."

"I hate it too." Mama fished around in the washtub.

"I swear, my blood runs cold every time that dead whistle blows."

"Mine too." Mama pulled out Daddy's blue-striped hickory shirt and spread it over the washboard. "That's why I can't help hoping you'll marry a man who goes to work sitting behind some nice, safe desk."

Storie blinked. It never failed to startle her when she realized how far into the future her mother was always looking. Personally, she couldn't begin to form a picture of this man behind a desk who she might want to marry.

"I'd hate to see you have to live like this," Mama went on, attacking the dirty ring on the shirt's collar with a stiff brush.

"But, Mama, I love it up here. It's *you* thinks I want to be down in some old fancy town, not me. I love the woods."

"I don't mean that. You want to live way up here, that's fine. I'm talking about the fear. What you were saying. Having to fear every day your husband'll get hurt."

"So you don't think it's true? That a man don't go till his time comes?"

"Oh, Storie, you're a smart girl. What do you think?"

What Storie was beginning to believe was not something they were supposed to say aloud: the more dangerous a man's job, the sooner his time would likely come.

"Logging's a cruel business," Mama said. "And the worst part is, loggers can't seem to give it up even when they try. I've seen men go to farming or leave to start up some little business. But they always come back. So you ought to have fair warning on this before you go sweet on some young choker setter."

"I ain't sweet on nobody. Don't plan to be, either."

"Oh, honey, you can say that, but you just don't understand how fast a handsome man can change your plans. I was all set to be a teacher when I met your daddy, you know."

"You were?"

"Oh, yes, because, you know, Grandma used to be a teacher and of course your aunt Dorothy. Then my friend talked me into that grange hall dance. I took one look at your daddy and that was that."

"Mama. You say that almost like you're sorry."

"No, of course not. Not sorry I married him. Your father is one of the best men God ever put breath into, and I'm proud to be the one who takes care of him. You've seen how it is when he comes home from work some winter days, wet to the skin while we've been sitting inside, warm and cozy. Seems little enough to have a fire going and a good meal for him. Usually I feel like I can't do enough for him, and I don't mind everything that's come my way from being his wife. I'm just sorry I had to make the choice about teaching, that's all."

"Well, why did you?" Storie thought of the teachers she'd had who'd been forced to quit when they married.

"I don't know. It's just the way they do it."

"I think it's stupid."

"Maybe, but it's the way it is. Anyway, I just want you to be careful. Don't be too quick to fall for some logger."

"But, Mama, who else is there to fall for up here?"

"Exactly. Why do you think I'd like to see you go to school down in Forest Grove? You might meet some nice college boy. Think of it—never having to listen for the dead whistle." She sighed. "Of course I've learned to deal with the fear better than I used to." She dropped the shirt in the rinse water. "Why, when we were first married, I used to walk your daddy to the crummy every morning and meet it every night. All day I'd wring my hands and half think he wouldn't be on it, come evening. 'Looky here,' says old Mrs. Bidwell, 'you're gonna jinx that good-looking man of yours right into an accident if you don't quit carrying on like this. He'll be out there worrying that *you're* worrying. He won't have his mind on his business and *that's* when he'll have an accident.' "

"Well, fine," Storie said. "Anybody knows it's easier to say 'Stop worrying' than it is to stop."

"I didn't say she stopped me worrying. But it did shame me from meeting the train every night, and if I stuck to my business at home, I found I didn't think nearly so much about it as I did if I just stood there, watching the tracks." She fed the shirt into the wringer. "That's why I try so hard to keep busy when something's scaring me."

"Don't seem like Daddy worries about getting hurt at all. He jokes about it. I've heard him with the other men."

"I know." Mama shook her head. "I s'pose they have to. Otherwise they'd be too scared to go out and get the job done."

"I think I'll just never get married at all," Storie said. "Then for sure I won't have to worry."

"Ha! Storie, one of these days somebody's going to look at you a certain way and that plan'll fly right out the window."

"You think so?"

"Yes, I do. And after all, you know what it says about two being better than one." She gazed off down the tracks. "Not to mention another very important thing."

"What's that?"

Mama turned back. "If you don't get married, how are you going to get yourself a daughter?"

For a short, shy moment they looked each other in the eyes. Then Storie had to glance away.

"Now." Suddenly Mama was all bustle. "Go hot me up some more wash water, will you? This has gotten cold."

Storie sat on the front porch that evening, stroking Patches, listening to the bell-chime song of a thrush in the forest. Thank goodness for the coolness of evening. The newspaper at the commissary said Portland had hit 102 degrees the day before.

Johnny and the others were up at the schoolhouse rope swing, and in the side yard the men were gathered around Daddy's chopping block as usual to pass tobacco and talk.

"I heard up at the store they figure that Hank

kid's gonna live," Rex Staver said. "Won't be doing no loggin' again no time soon, though."

"Never did no loggin' in the first place," Harly said. "Day one on the job."

"That's right," Rex Staver said. "Wadn't even here long enough to git told to dive in a hole if a log rolls. Tried to outrun it."

The men shook their heads.

"Only surprise," Daddy said, "is we don't have *more* broke bones, hiring these young apple knockers off the sidewalks of Portland."

"Ah, but that's what highball logging is all about then, isn't it?" Flynn Casey said. "Speed. Always pushing us to fetch out twice the sticks in half the time no matter how many men get hurt. And these short hoot-owl shifts just make it worse, taking on new ones."

Flynn Casey wasn't married but often came down to the family end of camp to visit. Storie had found she liked listening to him, liked to watch the way his dark eyes danced to the Irish lilt in his voice. Even if the things he said always did seem to make Daddy mad.

Actually, that's what Storie liked the most. Flynn Casey kept things interesting. Small and dark, he stood out among the Scandinavians. He had opinions about things, strong opinions he wasn't afraid to say right out loud. One time he declared they ought to be planting new trees every time they cut the old ones down. "Ha!" her father had fairly roared. "You let me know when they're paying the same for heeling in the babies as they are for taking down the grampas. I'll be first in line." That had won him a big laugh all around, but it didn't seem to bother Flynn.

"Young Flynn's got a point about accidents, Tom," Harly said now. "Sometimes I think I ought to vamoose on out of here myself while I'm still on my feet. Why wait for a stretcher ride down the mountain?"

"Three dollars and fifty cents a day," Daddy said. "That's why. Where you gonna find good pay like that these days? Where you gonna find a job at all? You been down to Portland lately? Got fellas down there doing odd jobs for nickels."

"That's just it, eh?" Flynn said. "They've got us trapped here, for what choice have we?"

Storie noticed that Alice was on her front porch, also keeping an eye on Flynn. One time she told Mama she'd asked him where an Irishman would get such dark eyes. "Says he got 'em from a Spanish sailor when the Armada shipwrecked offa Ireland. Now don't that sound kinda romantic?"

Mama had raised her eyebrows, and later made a point of telling Storie that a married woman had no business talking so free about the good looks of whatever eighteen-year-old boys were around.

"Is he only eighteen?" Storie asked.

"So he says."

"Talks older."

"Yes, well, I have the feeling there's more to his background than he lets on."

Now, down in the yard, Flynn braced his boot against a stump. "This is where the union could help us." He turned to Daddy. "And for the life a me, Tom, I can't understand why you're so set against it."

"I figure one boss is enough," Daddy said. "Don't need some union boss telling me what's what."

"But stickin' together we could change the rules," Flynn Casey said. "Force 'em to slow down the killin' speed."

Daddy snorted with disgust, and Storie guessed he was thinking what she'd heard him say a dozen times, that Flynn was nothing but a wet-behind-the-ears baby who thought reading a book or two made him an authority.

"Don't matter what kind of safety rules you make," her father said now, "cutting the big ones, a man's gonna go down once in a while. A man goes when it's his time, that's all."

Flynn shook his head, but good-naturedly, as if he'd had this argument before and expected to have it many times again.

"Anyway, son, loggers don't take to unions. We're all of us too ornery and independent-like."

They all chuckled in agreement at this, even Flynn. Then he glanced over and caught Storie's eye. He smiled and flicked off a wink.

Her father snapped to attention. "Estora Faye, git inside."

Now what'd I do wrong? she wondered, going in. Can't a girl sit out in the evening air and play with her cat a little?

Later, in bed, she overheard Daddy talking to Mama.

"I don't like that boy hanging around down here," he said.

"He's agitating for the union again?"

"Oh, his agitatin' is pretty tame. Not as bad as some of these soreheads."

Storie strained to hear above Johnny's soft snoring.

"No," her father went on, "it's the other bothers me."

"The other?"

"You got eyes in your head, Margie? If I remember anything about being eighteen, I'd say he's got his eye on a certain filly."

Storie's eyes went wide in the dark. Could this mean *her*? And then she heard her mother laugh.

"*I* remember *you* being eighteen."

"That's right, so you know exactly why he worries me!"

Storie picked her way down the tracks with the jar lids Mama had asked her to fetch from the store. She could hear Johnny and the other boys hollering way up on the creek trail, but the distant clank of the logging machinery was noticeably absent. Not that she'd ever actually liked the nagging squawk of the steam donkey's whistle, but she missed it now for what it would have meant—that a normal day's work was proceeding. The quiet was a reminder: the men had been sent off to the fire lines at Gales Creek.

"Estora Faye!" Mama hollered from the front door. "Hurry up! Let's get going on these beans."

Storie crossed the plank to the porch. "You know, Mama, I never thought about the logging noise till now it's gone." She followed Mama inside. "Remember that time back at White Star? We were standing on the back porch and you said, 'Hear that?' and I said, 'I don't hear anything,' and you said, 'That's what I mean. They're logging beyond that ridge now and it blocks the sounds. When you can't hear the logging show anymore, you know camp will be moving soon.'"

Mama took the lids from her. "You remember me saying that, hmm?"

Storie nodded. "You were right too." Not long after that they'd dragged the houses up onto flatcars and hauled them by rail to this new camp in deep timber. Storie hadn't minded one bit because by that time White Star was sitting in a vast wasteland of stumps. Without the forest, these mountains were nothing.

"Do you think the men are at the fire yet?" Storie said.

"Could be."

"How long you think they'll be gone?"

"I don't really know. It sounded like they thought they'd have it mopped up pretty soon."

"Hope so. This place feels emptier than last year's bird's nest." Storie plopped herself in the rocking chair. "I don't like it when Daddy's gone."

"Well, neither do I. Tell you what, let's just keep busy and time'll go faster."

Storie cast a mournful look at the burlap sack of green beans. "Do we have to can? Mama, it's already working up to a scorcher again."

"Now, Storie . . ."

"I'll bet this is gonna be the all-time worst day in the history of the world for putting up beans."

"Now look here, these are good Blue Lake pole beans and we ought to be grateful we *have* them, what with people going hungry right here in our own country. Besides, it's always hot in canning season."

"Not hot like this. Not hotter'n hollerin' hell."

"Storie! Watch your mouth!"

"Daddy says that. Why can't I?"

"There's lots of things your daddy says I don't want you saying."

"But—"

"Not because it's a privilege for him, but because I want better for you."

Storie slid down in the rocker.

"Your daddy's a good man, but his language— Well, up here it's fine, but, Storie, I don't like to hear you say 'ain't,' for instance."

"Oh, Mama . . ."

"Because I want you to be able to go down with the folks who *don't* say 'ain't.' "

"Who says I want to go down there?"

Mama sighed, putting water on the cookstove

to heat. "I just mean if you want to, you'll have that choice. You'll feel comfortable."

You mean *you'll* feel comfortable, Storie thought. You won't feel so ashamed of me. A few years back when there was a little more money, Mama had taken her into J. C. Penney's in Forest Grove. Storie hadn't wanted a new dress anyway and when she realized Mama was set on having her try on several, she'd rebelled.

"I ain't takin' my clothes off, no sirree!"

"Storie!"

The salesladies outside the dressing room tsked and murmured, and then Storie heard the three words that stood right out—*log camp kid.*

Well, she *was* a log camp kid, but something about the way they said it and the furious way Mama started tugging the dresses over her head made it plain these were dirty words. *Log camp kid.* She could still recall the feel of her mother's fingers digging into her upper arm as she was dragged from the dressing room, could still picture how Mama stuck out her chin at the saleslady as she slapped down money for a fancy dress Storie had ended up wearing only once or twice.

"I like to say 'ain't,'" Storie said now. "Sometimes 'ain't' is just the perfect way to put it."

"Oh, Storie . . . Now look here, I wouldn't say this to anyone but my own daughter, but you know how Jeannette Wicks asks me up to visit sometimes? You'll notice she doesn't ask Alice

Harlan. Speaking better really can open doors for you."

Storie nodded sullenly. It meant a lot to Mama to have Mrs. Wicks's door open to her, even if it was only the Wickses' summer residence. Their cottage was a wonder in the wilderness, with its glossy polished wood floors and paneling painted a soft cream color. Mrs. Wicks had chintz cushions with roses on them too. Stepping inside, Mama said, was almost like a little vacation from camp.

But after one peek to satisfy curiosity, Storie didn't care whether that door was open to her or not. She didn't have a clear picture of exactly which doors she *would* want opened.

And wasn't it funny, how Mama and Daddy were so different about this? While Mama wanted to figure how to make life's closed doors open, Daddy thought closed doors weren't worth opening and to heck with them anyway. He seemed to actually encourage any complaining Storie might care to do on the subject of Forest Grove or what life would be like down in the valley.

"And just think," Mama was going on, "speaking better doesn't cost a penny!"

"Oh, Mama, how you s'posed to change a habit of how you talk every single day of your life?"

"Well, it's not as hard as lots of other things. Can't change if you're short or tall, can't make yourself warble like a songbird if you're tone-deaf.

But, Storie, you make up your mind to stop saying 'ain't,' I have faith you can do it."

Storie chewed her lip. Actually, she figured she knew the right words. You couldn't read all the books she had and not get the picture. But what Mama didn't understand was that while highfalutin talk let you feel comfortable with some people, it made you *un*comfortable with others. People would laugh at you. Storie had already discovered this from trying out a fancy new word a time or two. "La-di-da!" the Staver boys had said. "Think you're better than us." She'd heard the men mimicking Flynn Casey for the way he talked too, never saying 'ain't.' She'd even seen the other mothers roll their eyes at Mama behind her back . . .

"And as far as these beans," Mama was saying, "just think how your grandma and Uncle Ralph troubled to get them all picked and put on the log train with the mail. Why, if she came up to visit and didn't find them all lined up in jars, I just don't know what I'd tell her."

Now there's a notion to weigh down your very soul, Storie thought, pushing herself up and tying on an apron. Mean to say that no matter how grown you get, you still have to worry about your mama's opinion of every little thing you do?

"We need to get these out of the way," Mama said. "Pretty soon they'll be sending up the prunes."

"Johnny!" Mama shouted. "Billy! You boys stop that!"

In the ditch along the rails, the two of them were rolling together in a dusty little punch fight. As Mama rushed to pry them apart, Storie saw her chance for escape.

She darted down the tracks and veered off into the deep shade of the creek trail. *Ahhh* . . . just getting under those old trees cut the heat considerably. She'd be in trouble for running off, but so what? She filled her lungs with the cool freshness. It was like a tonic, this air, laden with the sweetness of the lush creek-watered plants.

She set off walking, following the path a mile or more up to the place where the brook cascaded in a waterfall over a rock ledge, forming a lovely amber pool at the base. The boys preferred the deeper hole down closer to camp with the higher jumping rock, but this was the place she thought of as her own. Here the soothing sound of the tumbling water could even block the noise of the logging shay's whistle as it rumbled through camp.

It was like a private garden, she always thought. Not the picture-book kind with everything in tidy rows. But if you took time to notice, you'd find an order to the beauty. Hundreds of different plants grew in delicate balance, each in its own place, its own season, the sword ferns and trillium, tiny yellow Johnny-jump-ups and the shamrock-like sourgrass.

In spring, the pale white flowers of the dogwood caught the light streaming down above the pool, and in autumn, a branch of vine maple arched over it, dropping rusty red star leaves onto the water. Once last winter Storie had made her way up here to find icicles hung along the falls and every twig and fir needle edged in frosty white sparkles.

Now, in summer, it was all shades of green, the light filtering through the alder leaves and flashing golden on the water. Storie stood at the graveled edge of the pool for a moment, then waded in.

That anything could still be cold in this oven-hot, baked-out world struck her as purely miraculous. Cold, clear water, shaded by the towering firs. As she eased herself into the coolness, she thought fleetingly of peeling off her overalls. Didn't dare, though. She'd given up naked swimming since the day it turned out the Staver brothers had been watching her from the bushes. "We seen you!" they taunted her for weeks afterward.

After a while she pulled herself out, streaming water, and lay on her special wide, flat, sun-warmed rock. Her overalls would dry in no time.

She rested her cheek on one crooked arm and trailed the other in the water until she noticed a brown trout lazily circling. Then she carefully withdrew her arm to leave the fish undisturbed. She could lie that way all afternoon, she thought, just staring at the speckled creature, imagining its fish life.

This was something her father simply could not understand. Once when she'd talked about watching the fish up here, he'd said, "So, did you come back for a pole?"

"I just wanted to watch it," she said.

"Jumpin' devils! Fish are for catching, girl. What do you think God put 'em there for? Next time you see a fish, you get yourself a pole and bring home some dinner, you hear?"

Storie never ran home for a pole, but she never made the mistake of talking about watching fish again, either.

Now she lay by the pool as the sun moved lower in the sky, slanting shafts sparkling on the gurgling riffles and eddies downstream. She dreaded going home, figuring she'd be in trouble, but knowing the longer she stayed, the worse it would be. Finally she stood and took one last deep breath of it all.

FORTUNATELY, BACK AT camp she found her mother entertaining Jeannette Wicks.

"Storie!" Mama said. "My goodness, where have you been? Never mind, look what Mrs. Wicks has brought you." Mama held up something yellow —a dress.

"For *me*?" Storie said.

Mrs. Wicks nodded. "It was mine, but I never wear it. My sister-in-law gave it to me but, you know, yellow doesn't do a thing for me. The other day, when I saw you walking through camp, Storie, and realized how much you'd grown I thought, well, this would be perfect on you."

"Um, thank you." Storie tried to back away as Mama held it up to her. "It's . . . so long," Storie said.

"It's supposed to be," Mrs. Wicks told her. "It's the latest."

"Storie, won't you look up to date!" Mama

turned to Mrs. Wicks. "Isn't it a shame, though, how they had to drop the hemlines just when people don't have the money for extra fabric?"

"Yes," Mrs. Wicks said, although this could hardly be a problem for her. Mr. Wicks earned a good salary. "Aren't you going to try it on, Storie?"

"Now?"

The two women looked at each other.

"Yes, Storie," Mama said. "Now."

Storie went into the lean-to bedroom and slipped out of her stiff, sun-dried overalls. She pulled the dress on over her head.

"Need any help?" Mama called through the curtain.

"No, I can get it."

Was it really possible she could fill out a grown-up dress? The cotton fabric was light and floaty. The skirt fit smoothly over her hips, flaring at the bottom, and the top had little cape sleeves, which Storie thought were silly. But when she pulled back the curtain, her mother and Mrs. Wicks seemed impressed.

"Why, Margie, isn't that the most amazing transformation? It's as if she's been growing up on the sly."

"Oh, I've noticed," Mama said. "My, I would like to brush that hair, though. Did you go swimming or something, Storie?"

"That is the perfect color on her, isn't it, Margie? With her skin that golden shade? And her hair?"

"Now, Jeannette," Mama said, obviously pleased, "we can't have this going to her head."

"Oh, but she looks so beautiful! She's got to see herself." Mrs. Wicks glanced around. "We need a full-length mirror. Let's walk her up to my house so she can see."

Storie stepped back. "No!"

They blinked at her.

"I mean . . ." Storie faltered. "I don't want to walk outside in it. I might get it dirty."

Mama tilted her head toward Mrs. Wicks. "She is so shy lately."

"Oh, I see," Mrs. Wicks said. "But, Storie," she added, apparently gleaning the full implication of Mama's remark, "there are hardly any men left in camp. No one's going to see you."

A bit panicky, Storie glanced at her mother, hoping for sympathy. Mama would defend her against Alice Harlan's ideas for improvement, but it was different with Mrs. Wicks. Mama said Mrs. Wicks had good taste; she might make Storie cooperate.

But Mama said, "Well, I guess she'll just have to take our word for it how nice she looks."

"Woo woo!"

Storie whirled. At the window, Johnny and the Staver boys were peeking in.

"You get out of here!"

"Now, Storie," Mama said mildly, gliding out to shoo the boys away.

"Can I take it off now?"

Mama sighed. "Yes, go ahead."

As she pulled off the dress, she heard her mother murmuring to Mrs. Wicks in apologetic tones.

"Mrs. Wicks?" Storie said when she went back out. "Thank you very much for the dress. It's real nice of you to give it to me."

That part was true anyway, and it softened the look on her mother's face. Funny how much easier it was to be polite when she was safe in her overalls again.

SUNDAY, AUGUST 20, 10:00 A.M.,
TILLAMOOK

On Saturday evening, reports indicated that the great fire was close to being controlled, thanks largely to a cooling in the weather. This concerned the pastor of Tillamook's Savior of the Valley Church, who worried that the sermon over which he'd been laboring might be out of date by morning. A shame, for he truly felt it was one of his finest ever.

It was too late to write a replacement, he decided, so on that copper-hazed Sabbath he opened the Bible to Jeremiah, braced his hands on the pulpit and leaned forward with grim conviction.

" 'I will punish you according to the fruit of your doings, saith the Lord,' " he thundered, " 'and I will kindle a fire in the forest thereof, and it shall devour all things round about it.' "

The people blinked, amazed to hear these words straight from the Bible. Because wasn't it happening just that way? And as their pastor went on, citing other Bible passages, quoting Isaiah on the subject of God's retribution and His rebuke with flames of fire, they stole glances at one another and thought how true it was—all the wickedness afoot in the world these days.

But the room was so warm. As the sermon continued, people shifted on the hard pews. Thoughts began to drift.

A doctor mentally tallied the incredible number of tonsillitis cases he'd seen in the past week. People weren't meant to breathe this much smoke day in and day out.

A housewife wondered exactly how much longer the Lord planned for the fire to burn. Because she was just sick to death of trying to keep things clean with this everlasting soot sifting in through the smallest cracks.

And a little girl sitting in the back pew was repeating to herself one fervent prayer: Please don't let them cancel the Tillamook County Fair. Not after all the work she had put in, raising up that hog!

"Oh, Storie," Mama said. "A hike is the last thing I feel like doing."

"But I want to see for myself the fire ain't comin' this way."

Yesterday morning they'd heard the fire was almost under control, but another wind shift had driven it once more into fresh green timber, and now each whiff of smoke had Storie imagining the fire burning closer. It didn't help her jitters to have most of the men out of camp, either. What if the wind whipped the fire this way and Daddy wasn't here?

"Can't we just go up there and have us a look for ourselves?" she pleaded.

"Well . . ." Mama went to the front door. "Where's Johnny?"

"Down behind Stavers'."

"Oh, all right." Mama took off her apron. "But not because I'm worried. Only because I can see there'll be no peace sitting in this house with you if we don't."

They started out on the trail that ran in switchbacks up the mountain behind camp, swinging tin lard buckets for berries so Mama could feel the walk had some productive purpose.

"Looks like a fire all right," Mama said when they reached the viewpoint, a hot, huffing hour later. Smoke like dirty yellow cotton wool billowed above the horizon to the south.

"Oh," Storie said, relieved. "It *is* way over there, isn't it?"

"Looks about the same distance as the Cochran fire last year."

Storie counted three or four major ridges between them and the smoke. "I guess it couldn't ever burn clear over to here, could it?"

"I wouldn't think so," Mama said. "Especially with the wind pushing it west." She sat down on a huge stump. "So. Feel better now?"

Storie nodded, joining her. "Except for Daddy. You know, worryin' about him."

"He'll take care of himself. He's had to pitch in fighting lots of fires, you know. It's not like he's some CCC boy or one of these college kids they've got out there."

"Still . . . ," Storie said. Mama was probably scared for him too. She just didn't believe in saying it.

They sat in silence for a moment, surveying the surrounding valleys and ridges.

"Is that Saddle Mountain?" Storie asked, pointing to the northwest.

"Yes, North Saddle. South Saddle's down hidden in the smoke."

Storie studied the great chunks of land lying bare amid the green-clad mountains. "Gee, Mama, I never noticed before how much of this country already got logged off." The backside of the very ridge where they perched was a jumbled slope of waste wood recently left by another logging outfit.

The raw cut stumps showed these had been giant trees. Now the ground lay naked, exposed to a sun that baked the earth and killed off any living thing that loved the deep, damp shade.

"Looks like a battlefield, doesn't it?" Mama said.

Storie glanced at her mother in surprise.

"Don't ever put it that way in front of your daddy, though."

"Mama." Storie turned away. "I ain't stupid."

The tangled slash reminded her of the slope at White Star where she'd lost her secret glen, her *previous* special place. One day she'd been out rambling and realized she couldn't find the lovely spot where she liked to hide with a book. She'd stood disoriented on the cutover hillside until finally it dawned on her the glen was gone. It had simply been torn away, the entire hillside reduced to a swath of slashings, small trees chopped and laid waste in the fury of the logging, the haste to haul out only the biggest and the best.

"Those stumps look like paychecks to him," Mama said now.

Storie nodded. She understood that her father regarded a cutover hillside as a piece of hard and honest work completed, and never saw any contradiction in destroying the forest he loved. "That's what the trees are here for," he'd say. "That's what *I'm* here for. God made me a logger 'cause He knew I loved being out in the woods. I aim to make the best job of it I can."

And really, Storie thought, how could he look at it any other way when his gift was to look at a piece of forest and know how best to log it?

And the trees did go into the building of things, of course, things more important than a little girl's play place. Daddy bragged on the thousands of houses that had come out of this forest, the planes for the Great War that had been made from the Sitka spruce he felled down by Toledo.

No, Storie thought, you couldn't be crying over every log that bought your beans.

Still, she felt sorry about the creek at the last

camp, how it had turned brown during the first fall rain and filled with silt from the runoff.

"Mama," she said, "you really think these forests are going to be here forever like Daddy says? Because it looks to me like Sweetwater's about to meet up with those crews from Biggs and Bailey comin' over that ridge. And to the north you can see another outfit's workin' toward us from that direction."

Mama nodded. "If everybody wasn't shut down, I'll bet we'd be seeing donkey engine steam coming up out of every canyon."

"So *then* what are they gonna cut?"

"Well, Sweetwater has those holdings farther south, the ones Daddy and the others have gone to look after."

"Nobody's loggin' down there yet?"

"Oh sure, but not like here. That country's even more rugged, hardly any roads."

"But there's enough trees there to last?"

"Enough for our lifetime, anyway. Your father's knees'll give out before those trees do."

"But what about Johnny wantin' to be a logger?"

"Storie." Mama turned and leveled a look at her. "Why are you bothering yourself with this?"

"I don't know. It's just that Daddy's always said the trees'll last forever, but . . . what makes him so sure?"

Her mother got up and started picking blackberries. "Maybe because when *his* daddy started logging, it was such hard work getting those first big ones out, their last worry was cutting too fast. Probably pictured pulling every log out with a team of oxen, no idea how fast it'd go with a steam donkey engine and a railroad."

"But Daddy knows that now," Storie argued, following her. "He sees how fast they log a section and he *still* says they'll never run out."

"Well . . ." Mama shook her head and looked out over the patchwork slopes. "He worshiped his daddy, you know. That's probably what it boils down to. Papa Pete told him the trees would last a thousand years and that's what your father will believe until the day he dies."

Guilt pricked at Storie like a blackberry thorn. Did doubting her father mean she loved him less? Was she supposed to deny what she saw with her own eyes? She dropped a few berries into her pail.

"Maybe Daddy's countin' on it growin' again," she said, "and this cutover part'll go right back to forest. I mean, looky all these little baby firs a-springin' up."

"A lot of what comes up is alder, though, and that beats out the fir. This'll never be what it was. Not for years and years."

Years and years, Storie thought. Sad.

"But the forest *will* come back," she said, as if to convince herself. "Somehow. And Daddy probably knows better than we do, don't you think?" After all, her father was the smartest man in Blue

Star Camp. She had always taken on faith every last word he said.

It gave her an odd little ache, the thought of starting to doubt him now.

A giant thunderhead of smoke loomed above Gales Peak, and from it burning embers whirled up and outward and rained down into the parched grasses of the Tualatin Valley. Sirens whined continually as the Forest Grove fire trucks raced from one blaze to the next.

On a farm west of town, a set of twin boys were beating flare-ups with wet gunnysacks.

Thwap. "Wish we had shovels . . ." *Thwap* . . . "like the real fire crews." But the town's entire collection of shovels had been scoured from the hardware stores and sheds and sent up to the fire lines. Burlap would have to do.

"Over there!" One dashed for a spark.

Never in their eleven years had they worked so hard at anything, flailing those little fires into submission, their faces serious. Only once, briefly, did they stop, panting, and catch in each other's eyes a glimmer of something other than determination.

Guiltily, they glanced away. It wasn't right to be having fun, not with Mom jumping every time the phone rang, fearing bad news about their big brother, who'd been called back to the lines last night when the fire spread into the Scoggins Valley. Every family in town had somebody up there, and the women had run themselves ragged over the weekend, helping feed the crews who'd come down for some rest.

And as for Dad, his face this afternoon was grim. The town's whole future was going up in smoke out there right along with the timber, he said, the finest timber in the world, bar none.

The boys had no business enjoying themselves.

But the truth was, until last week, this vacation had been so boring. Now their quiet little college town was bustling with men. And real army trucks!

Besides, could they help it if spark chasing made a great game?

"There! By the fence!"

And the gunnysacks flew.

The men were home from the fire lines, and the women and children streamed up the tracks to meet them.

Never had the shay let off a more beaten-down-looking bunch. They were black with soot and stooped with defeat. Rex Staver limped.

Storie spotted her father and started to run, then stopped, struck by the strange look of his bloodshot eyes.

"Daddy," she said, stealing up to him. "Did you know your eyes are flat-out red? And your eyebrows—"

"Burnt clean off," Johnny murmured, impressed. "Boy howdy, you musta got awful close to that fire."

"Closer'n I like," their father said, exchanging a look with Mama, who reached out to touch one of the black spark holes burned into his shirt.

"We lost it all, Margie." His shoulders sagged. "All that fine Sweetwater timber."

Mama's answer was a sad look.

"Years of the best loggin' shows you ever seen, wiped out."

Mama slipped her arm around him.

"No, now look out, there," he said. "Don't wanna get you all dirty."

But Mama hung on. They turned and started for the house.

"I'm sure you and the other men did everything you could, Tom."

He shook his head with the hopelessness of it. "Ain't like fires I've seen before, just burnin' in the cutover stuff."

"Oh, Tom." Mama bit her lip. "You could've been killed."

"One barb-wire deal out there, all right. We got guys fought in France saying somebody give 'em a choice, they'd go back to the trenches before they'd put in one more minute on these fire lines."

No one spoke for a moment as they shuffled along; then Mama said, "Well, I'll bet you're hungry. We'll have something ready before you're even done washing up."

But he walked right past the washtub on the back porch and into the house. Storie and Mama looked at each other and followed him.

He fell on the bed in his dirty clothes and was instantly asleep.

"Well," Mama said softly. "Well. I never knew your father ever to come home more tired than hungry." She turned to Johnny. "Run on outside now. Let's leave him be."

"Mama," Storie whispered, "look at his hands."

Mama gently lifted and turned his raw, blistered palm. "Mercy. And those calluses he started with were tough as leather gloves."

Before long, the wives and children gathered on the tracks, in hushed voices trading bits of information the men had given before they'd fallen, every last one of them, into exhausted sleep.

"Harly says there's spot fires poppin' up all over," Alice was telling the others. "Looks like they're all gonna join up. Some fool camper over at Jordan Creek walked off and left his fire, now it's outta control. Got hundreds of men out there, but it just ain't enough to go around."

"Don't matter how many they put on the lines," Mrs. Staver said. "Some of that country down there's so rough—why, it'd take three days to hike in before a crew could even start to fight it, and if they hafta run for it, how the heck they gonna get out? Helpless as cattle at a barbecue."

Storie winced. Mrs. Staver had a voice like a rusty saw and she picked her words to match.

"Sure wouldn't want to be sittin' in Wheeler or Tillamook about now," Mavis Bunch said. "Jack says the fires are fixin' to sweep straight through to the coast."

"Yeah, and you ever been to Wheeler?" Mrs. Staver said. "Shoot, the trees come right down to the edge of town."

May LaBranche swallowed hard, and Alice took another nervous drag on her cigarette.

Mrs. Staver crossed her arms over her huge chest. "Say, sister, you gonna smoke them things around here, I hope you know how to put 'em out."

Alice raised her penciled eyebrows.

"You gotta spit on it, hear? Spit on it and grind it into the dirt. Not this here fluff on top—the real dirt underneath."

Alice went pink.

Nobody talked back to Ethel Staver. Of all the women, she'd been around the longest. She'd lived in a dozen different logging camps and was proud of not having a good word to say for any of them. A funny thing Storie had noticed, though—Mrs. Staver complained the loudest on her own front step, but it was Mama who'd march her hundred pounds up to Mr. Wicks's office and voice a formal complaint when necessary. It wasn't Mrs. Staver who'd got the company to install screens on the creek intake when they all got tired of frogs coming through the lines . . .

"They're tellin' people over there on the coast to pack it up," Mavis went on. "Get ready to leave."

"Probably wouldn't hurt us to get a few things packed up too," Mrs. Staver said. "Just in case."

May looked stricken. "It's not coming this way, is it?"

"No, no," Mrs. Staver said, patting her shoulder. "Now don't you fret yourself."

Alice made a big show of spitting on her cigarette and crushing it out. "Okay?" she said, with a half-nasty smile at Mrs. Staver.

"Good girl."

"Anyway," Alice said, "Harly says he has to admit them CCC boys are pullin' their weight just fine."

"Rex says so too," Mrs. Staver added. "Bless their hearts. Them poor boys, so far from home."

"Who's in charge of all this fire fightin' anyway?" Mavis said.

"Huh. The forestry folks, I s'pose," Mrs. Staver answered. "But I'll tell ya what. Sounds like a handful of ants runnin' around down at that ranger station. Rex says there's so much smoke they got two hundred square miles they don't even know where it's burnin' and where it ain't. Don't help that they're losin' the lookouts' phone lines."

"Two hundred square miles?" Storie said. "Can that be right?"

"Honey, would I lie? Like Alice said, we got all these separate fires, just a-joinin' up. I'll tell ya, the whole dang thing's started to sound exactly like another Yacolt."

A hush fell on the group.

"What's a Yacolt?" Johnny ventured.

"Little town up in Washington," Mama said.

"I know, but when you say, 'Sounds like a Yacolt.'"

"Well . . ." Mama glanced around at the other women, flustered now. "It was nineteen ought two—a very hot, dry summer—"

"Like this one?"

"Yes," Mama said. "Like this one. A lot of fires broke out. Not just here but clear up in Washington and all the way down to the California border."

"Wasn't just a forest fire," Alice threw in. "That fire ate up sawmills, little towns. Heck, my mama and daddy got burned right outta the log camp they—"

"Alice!" Mama interrupted, and shot a meaningful glance at Alice's own Davey, who'd gone bug-eyed.

He sidled up for a fistful of his mother's skirt. "Is a fire coming here?"

"Naw!" Alice said, but the women all shifted uneasily, and when Mrs. Staver said she was of a mind to do a little just-in-case-type packing, the group quickly dispersed.

"So, are *we* gonna pack?" Storie asked her mother, following her.

"We'll pack," Mama said firmly, "when it's *time* to pack." She went on ahead into the house.

Billy Staver came up behind Storie, smacking a stick along the rail for the fun he got from bashing things.

"My dad seen dead deer all over the place out there at the fire," he said. "Burned black and crispy."

Storie sucked in her breath. "No, sir! You're making that up." She felt as if he'd smacked *her*. "Deer are fast. They'd just run away. My daddy says so."

"Your daddy's lyin'."

She clenched her fists. A couple of years ago she would have decked him. Now it didn't seem fitting. And Billy getting a bloody nose wouldn't bring back any deer.

"He seen lots of 'em," Billy went on. "Baby ones too, just like that little pet you got out back."

"Well, what if he did," Storie said, realizing with a dull and awful certainty that Billy was telling the truth. She marched off, determined not to cry in front of him. What had she ever done to Billy Staver to make him be so mean, anyway?

She went around back, let herself into the fawn's pen, and gathered the animal into her arms.

"Oh, Snowflake . . ." She couldn't even say it, it was so awful. The idea of something so terrible happening to this little creature, this fawn with no mama to follow . . .

As she sat there in the dust, she didn't know

which way to aim her anger. At Billy, for telling? At Daddy, for lying? Or at the fire itself?

Oh, sure, the mothers could shield the little ones from the scary fire stories, but it was too late for her. She'd already heard them, stories that seemed safe to tell on rainy winter nights over a pinochle game, nights when people kept shifting closer to the woodstove and the world seemed so wet that burning trees could hardly be pictured, let alone feared.

She remembered one about a long-ago fire that killed more than a thousand people in some little Wisconsin milltown. The rest of the world never even noticed because the city of Chicago burned the same day. Only the loggers kept telling of the Peshtigo disaster, and brought the story west when they'd finished off the trees in the Great Lakes States . . .

And what about that fire in Minnesota, where the engineer ditched a flaming train of people in a lake? Her own grandmother, Daddy's mother, had ridden the train, and Daddy's older brother, Uncle George, the baby in her arms that day, had the white burn scars on his hands to prove he'd lived through it too.

And the big blowup in the forests of Montana and Idaho in 1910—those men in the mine shaft . . .

"Storie! Come on in and give me a hand." Mama grabbed the washtub off the back porch. "We need to set up a real bath for your daddy."

Storie stood and slowly brushed the dirt from her overalls. She didn't much care about talking to Daddy at all now. What was the use of asking a person questions if you couldn't count on truthful answers?

Mama marched in the front door and yanked
aside Storie's bedroom curtain. "Storie, put
on that yellow dress."

Storie lowered her Hopalong Cassidy novel.
"What for?"

"You have a job, my girl. Up at the cookhouse."

"Me? A job?"

"That's right. Earlene's run off with some fellow from Astoria and Bridey needs a quick replacement, what with the extra men for hoot-owl
shift and then schedules all thrown off with the

coming and going and fire fighting. So I offered you."

"But Mama, why me? I can't cook."

"Every other woman around here has a husband and kids to tend to. And Storie, *think*. We could use a little extra money."

"Money?"

"Well, of course. This is a paying job. A dollar a day, Bridey says. Now, isn't it lucky Mrs. Wicks gave you that dress?"

Storie groaned. "I have to wear *that*?"

"Well, what? You think you're going to wear those filthy overalls? Any woman who works up there wears a nice cotton dress, you know that. And you seem to find every excuse to keep from finishing the blue one."

Storie sighed and started putting on the dress.

"I don't think Daddy's gonna like this," she said as Mama brushed her hair. "Me workin' around all them men. You know how he's always tellin' me to steer clear a the bunkhouses."

"Well, that's just because he doesn't want you looking like you're asking for trouble." Deftly Mama began to plait the thick blond strands. "But nobody's going to think anything about you waitressing, or bother you, either. Those boys know how to mind their manners around women." She bound the braid end with a bit of ribbon and tugged it tight. "There. Now scoot."

Storie crossed the ditch plank. *Darn it any-*

way. She tried keeping her eyes on the railroad ties, but that didn't work—her feet looked so terrible! In a dress like this, a person ought to wear dancing slippers, not these clunky, worn-out lace-up shoes.

"Well, Estora Faye, look at you." It was Alice on her front porch, smoking a cigarette. "Where you off to in them caperin' clothes?"

"Goin' to work," Storie mumbled. "At the cookhouse."

"Well, that might be kind of fun, with all the fellas." Then Alice shouted back into her house, "Harly, come look. This is so cute. Little Storie next door's going off to work."

Storie hurried past the houses. Why was this so hard? She was no scaredy-cat. Hadn't she ridden on the shay's cowcatcher all the way down the mountain, careening around those curves and over the trestles, clinging for dear life? Right now she felt like she'd rather do that again any day. Anything instead of walking through Blue Star Camp in a yellow dress.

But . . . a dollar. Twenty candy bars. No, that wasn't right. A person earning grown-up money ought to have a more grown-up thought on how to spend it. But on what? Books? Tickets for the picture show at the Star when they visited down at Grandma's? Alice said *Forty-second Street* was terrific with all the tap dancing . . . But Mama probably planned to throw every penny in the family pot anyway.

As she approached the commissary, Jimmy Wicks stepped out onto the boardwalk and stood there blocking her path, staring.

"Uh, hi, Storie."

"Hi."

"Say, what—hey, is that my mother's dress?"

"It *was*." She stuck up her chin. "She give it to me."

He grinned. "Well, I didn't think you stole it. I just—it looks swell."

"Thanks." She dodged around him, blushing.

And then, in front of the cookhouse, under the iron triangle and gut hammer, she spotted Flynn Casey. Now he was the last person she wanted to see.

"Well, good morning, Miss Storie."

"Mornin'." Why did she have to all of a sudden remember what Daddy had said about him hanging around their end of camp?

"Ah, but you're looking lovely, I must say."

Was he making fun of her? She glared to get him to move. "Excuse me?"

"Oh, sorry."

He stepped aside and she hurried past him through the dining hall into the safety of the kitchen.

Whew!

Bridey, her new boss, was a white-haired woman with red cheeks.

"Wonderful!" she cried at the sight of Storie. "Our extra hands. We're saved." She shoved a starchy apron at Storie. "Don't s'pose you know anything about cooking."

"Well . . ." Storie was still a bit breathless, looking around, taking in the long, wood-burning range, the walls lined with shelves full of bowls. "My daddy says I make a pretty fair pie."

"Pie! Good! You can get started on tomorrow's lunch table pies. 'Course I don't know if we'll actually be laying a lunch-packing table tomorrow with this fire and who knows what going on, but we can feed 'em pies either way." She steered Storie to a big wooden counter covered with white canvas. "Here's the crust fixin's, here's the recipe." She tapped a paper tacked on the wall.

> *25 lbs. of flour*
> *1 cup salt*
> *2 cups sugar*
> *15 lbs. lard*

Lucky she was good at math, Storie thought. All she needed to know was how to cut this.

"Um, do you want I should divide it by ten or what?"

"Divide it? Honey, make the whole thing. We need fifteen pies here."

Fifteen!

"We'll do the cakes and cookies later."

WEDNESDAY, AUGUST 23, 12:00 NOON,
BLUE STAR CAMP

Storie circled the gut hammer around the iron
triangle, wincing against the clang. Down the
tracks, bunkhouse doors banged open and a stampede of men raised a dust cloud. Jumpin' devils!
She'd heard this thundering commotion from the
distant safety of her own house down the tracks,
but she'd never before been the one standing
smack in the way of it. She ducked back into the
kitchen.

"Bridey, you should see 'em comin'!"

"Oh, I know! Ever hear that old joke about the
logger who trips and falls, running to the dining

hall? He gets up, he just turns tail for the bunkhouse. 'Too late for me, then,' he says. 'Grub'll be all ate up 'fore I get there.' "

"That's no joke," Storie said, taking up three gray graniteware coffeepots in each hand and pushing open the swinging door to the hall with her hip.

She rushed in and out of the kitchen bearing huge trays of sandwiches and biscuits and pitchers of milk to fuel the fifteen-minute feeding frenzy the loggers called lunch. Occasionally, reaching around to set down a refilled plate in front of a man, she'd catch him glancing up at her with a certain interest, grinning shyly, maybe nudging the man next to him to check out the new waitress. But she was too blamed busy to worry much how she looked in her yellow dress or get flustered over Flynn Casey, watching her from spot twenty-three. Boy howdy, these men could eat!

"Truly, I never seen the beat," she said as Wanda handed her a freshly heaped tray of sandwiches.

When the men trooped out, Wanda and Storie gathered the dishes for old Ned, who did the washing. After that they swept, and Wanda showed her how to clean and refill each table's setup—a collection of salt, pepper, catsup, steak sauce, bread, butter, jam and jelly—and cover it with a white flour sack to keep out the dust until the next meal.

As soon as the tables were reset, it was time for potato peeling.

"We figure a pound a day per man," Bridey told Storie, sitting her down on an empty blasting-powder box next to Wanda in the storeroom, handing her a knife and a dishpan to balance in her lap.

As Bridey bustled back and forth in the kitchen, they chatted through the open doorway.

"I tell ya," Bridey said, "I am wore out with this business of havin' the men in camp all hours, sniffin' around for food, gettin' underfoot. I was so tuckered out last night, I got back to the flunky shack, lay back on my cot without even gettin' undressed—next thing I know, the alarm's goin' off and it's mornin'. Time to go to work again. Ain't that so, Wanda?"

Wanda nodded. "She's too soft on 'em," she said to Storie. "First it was 'make 'em wait.' Now she's got me laying out cookies and such all day long and keeping the coffeepots full. How we supposed to get the next meal on?"

"Oh, I know I shouldn't." Bridey shook her head. "But I can't help it. To me they're all just a buncha lost boys in men's clothes. Mind you, I ain't arguin'. I'd like 'em outta my hair same as you."

"It was okay while they was all still dead tired from fire fighting," Wanda said, "but now they're waking up, roaming around camp, picking fights . . ."

"Already a couple of poker games goin', I hear," Bridey said. "Bad sign. These young fellas, you gotta keep 'em busy or they go haywire. Mercy! I sure do wish it would rain."

Storie sighed in agreement.

" 'Course I guess this still ain't nothin' to the Silverton fire in sixty-five," Bridey went on. "My granddad used to talk about that one. And I'll never forget the Yacolt." She shuddered.

"You were in it?" Storie said.

"Well, not *in* it, girl, or I wouldn't be here. Ran from it, though. Oh, it was terrible. Buncha picnickers got caught—kids and all—came so fast they didn't have a chance. And a woman with her kids, hidin' in her basement? Whole thing crashed in on 'em."

Storie's knife stopped, mid-potato. "Oh, Bridey."

"Yes, and then the poor soul—friend of my mother's—who died tryin' to save her prize Singer sewing machine."

"What!" Storie said. "Now that is something you will never see me give my life for!"

"One time," Wanda said quietly, "the whole world was on fire."

Storie and Bridey stopped and looked at her.

"My great-grandmother saw it. Back when she was young."

"Come again," Storie said. "The whole world?"

"Seemed like it to the people of my great-grandmother's tribe, the Alseas. The forests burned for weeks. The sky was black and the people ran down to the beaches to get away. The animals were there too. The bear, the elk and the cougar—all the wild creatures standing in the surf with the people, just watching the fire over the mountain and waiting for it to run out of trees to burn. It burned way down to the lands of the southern tribes."

"But wait a minute . . . it couldn't have burned around here, or our trees wouldn't be so big, right?"

"Well, it was mostly farther down to the south." Wanda dropped a curl of potato peel into the bucket. "And don't forget, a forest fire's a strange thing. It can skip trees, leave some standing while others burn. You get a lot of trees on fire, you don't know which way it's gonna go."

"How come I never heard about this," Storie said, "if it was such a big deal?"

Wanda shrugged. "It happened before very many white people came here. Before they started writing down every last thing. The Indians told stories out loud and passed them on. My great-grandmother was known for her story of the great fire. By the time she was old they had added it to her name—*She-who-saw-the-flames!*"

"I've heard old-timers talkin' about that fire," Bridey said. "I put in a few years down there by Hebo. You can still see the stumps."

Storie was thinking of that long-ago girl, cooling her toes in those long-ago waves, watching the sky thunder and blaze.

"Anybody know how it started?" she asked.

Wanda shook her head. "But you know, I've heard they used to set fires on purpose, the Indian people did. Made for better hunting, keeping the undergrowth down."

"You know it wasn't set by no loggin' show, anyway," Storie said. "I guess there's always been fires, loggers in the woods or not."

The other two nodded.

Storie wondered if forests had a time to burn just like Daddy said a man had a time to die.

"Well," she said at last, "I got absolutely *no* hankerin' to be called *She-who-saw-the-flames!*"

"Okay, then," Bridey said, "we got all these pie crusts to fill. You can be *She-who-peels-the-apples.*"

"**H**ear you did good up at the cookhouse today,"
Daddy said to Storie that evening.

She shrugged, fanning her book's pages.
Sometimes a kind word made her feel just as shy
as a sharp one.

"Fact is," Daddy said, "Bridey's let on she
hopes you can go to work full-time one of these
days."

"Tom!" Mama dropped her sewing in her lap.
"And stop her schooling?"

"She's got enough, don't she? She does her

numbers. Reads and writes better'n me. Look at her—every time I try talkin' to her she's got her nose in some book." He grabbed the volume from her. "Now what the heck is this one?"

"It's called *The Good Earth*," Storie said. "It's about people in China."

"China! What do you need to know about that for? This is just foolishness." He tossed the book aside.

Storie cringed. Daddy sure knew how to pick a fight—calling books foolish right to Mama's face.

But with great control Mama lowered her eyes and went back to the hemming of Storie's blue dress. "I'd just like to see her get further than I did."

"And what's wrong with where you got to? You're eatin', ain't you? You got a roof. Plenty of folks'd be grateful for that about now."

"I am, Tom. You *know* I am."

"Maybe you're wishin' you were teachin' school like your sister, collectin' useless coupons instead of money."

Mama stiffened. "I'm sure her school district will pay when they can, but—now really, this has nothing to do with my sister. I just think Storie's a girl who . . . well, Miss Fowler, her teacher, says she's—"

"Miss Fowler! Storie's our girl, not hers." He turned to Storie. "How's chances, honey? Wouldn't you like a real job in the cookhouse where you could earn you a little money? Jobs don't come that easy these days, but I've got some pull with Wicks and I think I could get you on."

What could she say?

"Well, girl?"

Storie looked first to her mother, then at her father.

"Darn it, Margie, does she have to look at me like that with them yellow cougar eyes of hers?"

Storie glanced away, stung. She'd always thought he liked her eyes. But Daddy could get touchy about lots of things on a stifling August night, especially if he hadn't been able to do any logging that day.

"She goes down to your mother's place," he said, "we've lost her. Ain't just the schoolin'. It's everythin' that goes with livin' down there. Nothin' but city slickers and farmers."

"Oh, Tom . . ."

"And besides, your mother'd spoil her and who knows what-all nutty revolution-type ideas your brother'd put in her head."

Mama set her jaw. "Why do you always bring up that silly revolution business? Ralph never said that."

"Well, what do *you* call it, camping out on the White House lawn? The more you stir it, the more it stinks."

"They weren't on the lawn and you've got no business calling Ralph a traitor. Didn't I read you about that battle in the Argonne Forest?"

Storie eased the book off the table and took a backward step toward the door. She was beat on her feet from her day at the cookhouse and all she wanted to do was sit down and read *The Good Earth*.

"And why do you always have to say 'farmer' like it's a dirty word?" Mama asked. "You can't eat logs, you know."

Storie edged back another step as Daddy ignored Mama's remark and instead started arguing he'd never used the word "traitor."

Storie's hand reached back for the doorjamb. One more step . . .

"Now hold on," Daddy said, catching her. "Forget your brother," he said to Mama. "Let's get this straight about our daughter here. What do you say, girl? About the cookhouse flunky job?"

"Well . . ." Storie looked from one parent to the other. "Bridey and Wanda are real nice, but . . . the thing is, I really don't much like to cook."

Her father jerked back like she'd smacked him. "Gosh-o-hemlock! Whoever thought of likin' or not likin' it? Gotta be done, don't it?"

Lots of things in the world have to be done, she thought. That doesn't mean they have to be done by me. She didn't dare say this to his face, though.

"Honey," he said now, softening his tone, "you don't want to grow up to be no can opener artist. There's a reason loggers call a good meal 'bait,' you know. Heck, good cookin' is one of the most important things there is. I've seen loggin' outfits go bust for lack of a good cook to keep loggers in camp. Now didn't your mama here ever tell you that the way to a man's heart is through his stomach?"

Storie gave her mother a sidelong glance. "Yeah, she told me."

"Well, then."

"So what about Alice Harlan? She don't cook much and Harly seems to like her fine."

Some look went between her parents.

"Huh," Daddy grunted. "You don't want to be like Alice."

Well, that was true, although Storie suspected her reasons weren't the same as her father's. It all made you wonder, though—did Daddy figure men just went around marrying the best cooks they could find?

"Jimmy Wicks says if I ever marry him we can live in town and eat at a cafe every night." Saying this set her cheeks blazing. She wasn't good at lying. Actually this was what Jimmy said he planned to do if he *never* got married.

"You better keep clear of Jimmy Wicks," Dad said.

"Why?"

"He ain't your kind."

"Who *is* my kind, then, Daddy? Just tell me."

"Well! Since when did you get to be such a smart-mouth?"

She bit her tongue. She'd lay down money she

could sort through every living person in Blue Star and not come up with one he thought fitting for her to mix with. What was she supposed to do, just be his little girl forever? Seemed like every day made it plainer that this wasn't one of the choices.

"You think hard about that job," he said, and stomped off to bed.

THURSDAY, AUGUST 24, 5:30 A.M.,
ON THE KILCHIS RIVER

On a Kilchis River dairy farm just north of Tillamook, a young wife shut off the alarm and lay a moment, dozing. Then her eyes popped open. Was that what she thought it was? *Oh, thank you, God.*

She rolled over and squeezed her husband's shoulder. "Ben! Listen. *Rain.*"

What a welcome sound, that gentle rooftop patter. Blessed, blessed rain. The rain that could stop the fire faster than a million men with shovels. Rain that would wash the gray pasture grass green again.

She flung back the thin summer quilt, jumped out and fairly danced down the hall. She wanted to feel the wetness of it on her face, whirl in it until her nightgown clung coolly to her arms and legs.

But the front door opened to the same acrid air they'd been smothered with for days. She hesitated, then plunked barefoot down the plank steps into the yard, lifting her face and palms. What *was* it, falling from the darkness? Stooping, she raked the dry grass with her fingers and came up with a handful of something crunchy and forest-scented.

Fir needles. She raised her eyes to the sky like a child who's asked for bread and been given a stone. Spreading her fingers, she let the prickly bits sift through. Then she sank to the steps.

The screen door creaked. Her husband stepped out with a lantern.

"Fir needles." She spat the words.

He clumped down and scooped a handful, inspecting them in the lantern light.

"Huh. Not hardly burned." He looked to the east. "Must be a heck of a wind from that fire, carrying off everything." He stood in the yard a moment, staring into the darkness. Finally he shook his head. "Worst excuse for a summer mornin' *I* ever seen."

Sighing, his wife pushed herself up and went in to dress.

Because rain or fire, dawn or dark, the cows still had to be milked. If they could give milk, that is, with nothing to graze on but ashes.

The sun rose red, slanting its rays through a narrow clear band above the eastern ridges, then went coppery as it moved up into the dirty sky. Storie was giving her face a quick splash in the privacy of the back porch, getting ready to head up to the cookhouse.

Mama came out with her new blue dress. "All fresh-pressed."

"Oh, Mama, thanks." She gave her mother a shy glance. "Sorry I didn't finish up the sewing myself."

"Never mind. Maybe you weren't meant to

sew. And who knows? Could be someday you'll have enough money you can buy your dresses ready-made."

"I guess," she said, whispering on account of Daddy still sleeping. He didn't have to get up because it had already been decided: no logging today.

"You know, I was thinking," Mama said, helping her on with the dress, "if you ended up earning enough from this job, we might take a special shopping trip down to Portland."

Storie nodded, but only because she'd had her fill of arguing last night. What did she want with Portland? "You'll love it," Mama'd told her that other time, but Storie hadn't loved it one bit.

The place had been full of more people than she'd ever imagined in the world, most of them looking sad. While her mother peered in the shop windows and marveled at the low prices, Storie eyed the beaten-down men shuffling along and wondered why she and Mama had even come. What difference did low prices make if you didn't have money anyway? The city was noisy, a confusion of car horns and brakes and the voices of odd characters who stood on the corners, yelling at people to hurry up and get saved from hellfire.

She didn't care for the whole idea of sidewalks either, the hard jarring that ran up her shinbones and made her tired in just a few city blocks, she who could walk miles with ease on the cushiony duff of the forest floor.

Daddy'd laughed when she'd climbed down from the shay complaining about that. "Why, honey, you're sidewalk sore, just like any old logger who don't show his face in town but once every six months when he's stakey. Just shows you're a true logger's daughter."

She'd always liked him saying that, but now she had to wonder: maybe being a logger's daughter wasn't so good if it meant her only choice was working in the cookhouse. Not that the job itself was so terrible. She actually felt glad this morning to be going off to work that had such a clear purpose. And it wasn't like she had a firm plan of something she wanted to do instead. But inside, it gnawed away at her—the thought that, whatever she did, she sure ought to have more choices about it. Choices, and a chance to make up her own mind.

She turned so that Mama could brush and pin up her hair.

"I *am* gonna have to go to school down somewhere else, right? After this year?"

"Well, yes, unless you quit."

"No, I don't want to quit. I want to read more books." She hesitated. "Mama, I might even want to go to college."

The brushstrokes stopped a moment. "Then you'll *go* to college," her mother said, resuming.

"Daddy'll never let me."

"Oh, we'll see about that."

She stood there, braced against the strong, sure pull of Mama's brush.

"Why's he like that?" she whispered after a moment. "I mean like he was last night."

"Oh, Storie . . ."

"He gets so mad about nothing. It's got so I feel like I did some big sin when he catches me readin' a book even."

"Well, I think it scares him."

"What? Mama. Daddy ain't a-scared of anything. You know that."

"I know no such thing. Everybody has things they're scared of. Just comes out different ways in different people."

"But scared of books?"

"Sweetheart, when you were little, you thought your daddy hung the moon. Thought he had all the answers. But as soon as you started reading books, your questions got tougher. I'm sure that bothers him."

"But I never—"

"Hold still now." She opened a bobby pin with her teeth and anchored it in Storie's twist. "He sees you lost in a book and he knows you've gone off someplace he can't follow. He's probably afraid that when you figure out he doesn't have all the answers, well, then you won't love him anymore."

"Mama! That's—"

"Hold *still*."

"That's silly."

"I know. And he'll understand someday. But right now it's just hard for him, watching his little girl grow up."

Storie sighed and then laughed shortly, reaching up to feel what her mother had done with her hair. "I'll tell you, Mama, ain't no picnic being the one doin' the growin', either."

Forty-eight flapjacks—that's how many fit on the cast-iron griddle. By the time you got those poured out the first ones needed flipping. Wanda showed Storie how to go right down the line—flip flip flip.

"You catch on quick," Wanda said.

"Darn sight quicker than Earlene," Bridey agreed.

"Well, *Earlene*," Wanda said. "She had other things on her mind."

"Not only that," Bridey said, "but anybody'd

quit a job in times like these has to be crazier'n an outhouse rat."

"You said it," Wanda agreed. "Ain't like it was back when I started in twenty-seven. Times was good then, see, Storie. You could get a job anywhere. You didn't like the head cook who bossed you, just walk out, go to another camp. These days, you're stuck."

"Now just a dang minute," Bridey said.

Wanda grinned. "Lucky we get along, huh? Okay, now, see here, little flunky junior—every couple batches you want to take this burlap rag and wipe down the griddle with this here lard, okay?" Then she headed out to sound the wake-up call on the triangle.

It was true, Storie had learned a lot already. Not just about cooking and cleanup, but tricks to help shovel the food out there faster, how to balance five loaded plates on your left arm and one on your right, for instance, and the fastest route to swoop through the tables collecting the empties to refill in the kitchen.

But most interesting was learning there were worse things than being seen and admired in a yellow dress. The furtive glances and shy smiles of the young loggers made her feel . . . appreciated.

When Bridey and Wanda were ready to face the stampede, they sent Storie out to bang the triangle the second time, and within sixty seconds she was passing plates of bacon, hash brown potatoes, boiled eggs, fruit, hot buttered toast, doughnuts, rolled oats and of course all those flapjacks.

"Ain't like they're even going out to work today," Storie exclaimed in the kitchen, grabbing two fistfuls of coffeepots.

"Gotta fuel up for the poker games," Wanda said, flipping more flapjacks.

Storie was starved herself by the time the cookhouse staff got a chance for a bite of breakfast themselves. Eggs cracked between flapjacks and smothered in butter and syrup tasted awful good.

While they were eating, Mr. Wicks came in and told them the governor had forbidden logging across four counties, so they should figure on serving three meals each day in the dining hall until further notice.

"Oh, have mercy!" Bridey said. "Can't you send them off to fight the fires somewhere? We're plumb wore out here."

"Hate to send 'em too far off, Bridey. Way this thing is going, we might need 'em closer to home."

After cleanup, Bridey told Storie to take a break. "Step outside, honey—get yourself some of that good air!"

Very funny, of course, for the sky still hung thick and close with smoke.

Outside, a group of men hung around the commissary door, listening to the radio, trying to catch the latest news.

In Tillamook, two thousand new men had

headed up to the fire lines while the townspeople went to their churches in the ashy darkness of noon and prayed for rain. Families streamed down from their little stump ranches with whatever they could grab and pile on their trucks. A mill up on the Yamhill had apparently thrown off a spark and burned to the ground.

Storie wandered down to the place where the boardwalk ended at the cookhouse wood yard. There she sat, wondering again about the inevitability of forest fires. Sure, there were fires from lightning, and it was nature making the conditions so ripe for it right now. But these sparks— from a mill, a logging operation, a careless camper —these sparks would never have been struck without people in the woods.

At the sound of footsteps behind her she turned and found Flynn Casey.

She jumped up, ready to flee, but he braced his arm against the cookhouse, blocking her way.

"Now don't run off and leave your nice shady spot," he said. "I just wanted to ask how you're farin'." He looked over his shoulder. "If I can get away with that while your daddy's not around."

She blushed, eyes fixed on the bicep that rounded out the faded blue of his shirtsleeve. She hardly knew whether to smile or toss her head and walk away.

"That man guards you like a treasure, doesn't he? And well he should, for what are you now, just fifteen?"

"No, fourteen." She shifted uneasily, an odd warmth moving through her. *A treasure . . . he called me a treasure.* "Well, fourteen next month."

He laughed. "Oh, I'd better watch myself."

Suddenly she wished she had on the yellow dress instead of this homemade blue one. She felt prettier in the yellow.

"Thirteen. I suppose your father wouldn't even want me talkin' to you, then."

"That's okay," she said impetuously, looking him in the eyes, suddenly aware that he was not that much taller than she. "He ain't the—" She hesitated. "I mean, he isn't the boss of me."

"Well, now." He grinned.

He likes me, Storie thought, amazed.

"So how is it, workin' for Bridey?"

"She's nice to me," Storie said. "I'm gettin' along as good as can be expected. Considerin'."

"Considerin'? . . ."

"Considerin' we're all sittin' here chokin' to death on smoke. Considerin' nobody seems to know what's gonna happen from one day to the next."

"Nobody *ever* knows what's going to happen from one day to the next."

"Yeah, well, I've seen days more predictable." She relaxed a bit, looking out over the hazy brown mountains. Talking to Flynn wasn't as hard or scary as she'd imagined.

"So you're tired of the smoke, eh?"

She nodded. "Before this, I always liked the

smell of wood smoke. You know, in the winter, comin' from the cabins. Now I wonder if I'll ever like it again."

"We've surely had our fill."

Storie sighed. "I have never wanted it to rain so bad in my life! Lately I'm even *dreamin'* about it. I dream I'm lookin' up and feelin' it pour down all over me and it's so wonderful . . . Then I wake up."

"Ah, yes. I've had the same dream." He looked to the smudgy sky.

> *"Oh Western wind, when wilt thou blow*
> *That the small rain down can rain?*
> *Christ, that my love were in my arms*
> *And I in my bed again!"*

Now he was looking straight at her.

The warmth from her middle rushed straight to her head. She looked at him through a blur, without breathing, for what he'd said, and how he'd said it, his dark eyes going right through her like that . . .

"I . . . I better go." She glanced back once to see his eyes still on her, then turned and hurried up the wooden walk.

At the cookhouse door, Wanda cocked her head. "Was that Flynn Casey out there with you?"

Storie nodded, head down, trying to get in past her.

"Storie, what did he *say* to you?"

"Nothing. Just a poem or something. I don't know."

That was the truth. It had all gone by so fast and shocking.

"Bridey!" Wanda said. "That Flynn Casey's pitching woo at our Storie Faye here."

"Oh, Lord have mercy! That boy's got more charm in them twinkly dark eyes."

"I don't think he's so charming," Storie said, but her cheeks felt hotter than a fired-up griddle.

"Oh, honey," Bridey said. "You just better watch out!"

**THURSDAY, AUGUST 24, 4:04 P.M.,
YAMHILL**

Behind a house in Yamhill, a little boy ambled down the orchard path, the sharp smell of smoke in his nostrils mixing with the hot sweetness of windfall Gravenstein apples baking in the brown grass.

What a funny orange light, he thought, noticing the fuzzy shadows of the trees. Must be that big fire. They'd been watching the smoke over the coast range all week. He scuffed along to the wooden fence, where he liked to stand on the bottom slat and look out across the sloping fields.

But today at the fence, his breath stopped. He

gripped the top rail. To the northwest, over the mountains, a huge brown cloud of smoke was boiling up in the shape of a mushroom.

"Mommy?" he said softly, forgetting she was back at the house. Remembering, he dropped off the fence, turned and ran. "Mommy! Come quick!"

His mother pushed open the screen door, wiping her hands on her apron. "For goodness' sake, what is it? You know I'm up to my elbows in applesauce."

He stared at her, finally managing a vague wave to the west. "You better come." He grabbed her hand and tugged her through the orchard toward the fence.

And there she stopped. "My Lord."

The terrible cloud was billowing higher and spreading out, the dark bottom a dull red reflecting flames below.

He watched her press one hand to her chest and the other over her mouth. He felt a tiny thrill of satisfaction. He'd been right to fetch her. He turned back to the raging sky.

"Daddy said it would be out by now. He read me that from the paper way last week."

His mother simply stared at the monster cloud.

"Mommy, what if there are people up there right now?"

"Oh, no, honey," she said faintly. "I'm sure they told everyone to get out days ago."

Storie pushed open the cookhouse kitchen door
with an armload of wood just in time to hear
Bridey murmuring in such low, grave tones that
she knew at once something terrible had happened.

"What?" she said. "What is it?"

Bridey and Wanda turned to her.

"The fire blew up," Wanda said.

"Blew up? What do you mean?"

"Mr. Clinkinbeard just come down and tell
us," Bridey said. "He's listenin' on the radio. It

just . . . exploded. Came together in a huge whooshing rush. Got a cloud up there forty thousand feet high. It's like . . . well, it's like nothing folks ever seen before."

"A giant, eighteen-mile wall of flames," Wanda said, "just a-racin' for the ocean. Burned up more since this morning than it has in the ten days since it started."

"Well!" Storie dropped the wood in the wood box. "*Now* can we call this the worst fire ever happened around here?"

Bridey shook her head. " 'Spect so."

"And we're gettin' outta here, right?"

Bridey lifted her shoulders. "Not till somebody says so. Not till somebody give the word to fire up the train."

"Still ain't headed our way," Wanda said. "Long as it blows east and west we're okay, sitting north of it."

"Oh, I hate this!" Storie flung out her arms and started whirling around the kitchen, wheeling and smacking against the tables and walls like a trapped bird. "Why can't we just leave?"

"Now take it easy, honey," Bridey said, catching her, stilling her. "We got a job to do here. Whatever happens, these men are gonna need their dinner."

Storie burst out laughing, sinking to the floor against the wall.

Wanda peered at her. "She laughin' or cryin'?"

"Both," Bridey said.

Isn't this just always the way? Storie was thinking. The whole world can be burning up, and women's work goes right on. Just shut up and cook that food.

Strange. On the other side of the kitchen door, the dining hall had gone quiet. Bridey, Wanda and Storie looked at one another.

They pushed open the swinging door to find Mr. Wicks, the superintendent, in the middle of an announcement.

". . . broken out over there in some of the Oregon-American holdings, they're saying seven miles southwest of Vernonia."

"And how far from here?" somebody asked.

"If it's where I'm thinking, just a few miles. Reports have it at about three hundred acres."

A new fire, then.

"Oh, dear," Bridey said from the doorway behind Storie.

Men pushed up from the tables, but Mr. Wicks motioned them back down.

"Finish eating while we fire up the shay. Might be the last good meal you get for a while."

Sixty seconds later, plates were cleaned. Storie stood, shocked, as the men thundered by her.

"You be careful," she blurted at Flynn Casey.

He winked and ran.

She dropped onto a bench. Now why had she said that to him? And after making a point of avoiding his eyes all through lunch and dinner too.

Wanda handed Storie a tin pan for collecting dirty dishes.

In a daze she stood, balanced the dishpan on her hip and started gathering up the heavy china cups. Was this what war would be like? The men run off, all hopped up and ready to fight, and the women stay behind?

To wait and worry and wash the dishes.

It wasn't until the shay's whistle blew and it was too late to run out and say goodbye that she remembered: it wasn't just Flynn going off into danger—Daddy was on that train too.

After cleanup, Storie hurried out into the deserted camp and turned for home. There she stopped, struck by the sight of three empty flatbed cars parked on the tracks between the houses.

" 'Bout time, doncha think?" Mrs. Staver called from her porch as Storie came down the track. "I's beginning to think they was planning on waitin' for our apron strings to catch fire 'fore they give a thought how to get us outta this dump."

This was it, then. Blue Star was readying for possible evacuation. Storie stared at the flatcars, uncomfortably reminded of the story Uncle George told about the forest fire in Minnesota and the train that was burning even as they rode it away.

She found her mother stacking packed orange crates by the door.

"Oh, Mama."

"Now don't get upset, Storie. It's just a precaution. I've been packed to run from fires before. Never had to yet."

Storie got out of her dress and into her overalls. Then she paced the house. *Get ready, get ready* . . . but how? Mama had already boxed up the books, the only thing Storie'd been worried about saving. The only nonliving thing, that is.

Looked like once again she was left with the worst part, the waiting.

She dropped beside the box of family pictures Mama had put out—brownish portraits of grim people with hair parted in the middle and oiled down.

"Just about everything else in this house we could replace," Mama said. "But not these."

Patches rubbed against Storie as she began to sort through them. Here was one of her grampa, Papa Pete, posed next to the stump of a huge tree he'd felled. In another he struck a cocky pose, stretched full-length in the cut-out notch of a giant that hadn't gone over yet. What an earthquake it must have made when it did, Storie thought.

She held it next to one of her mother's mother as a young woman. She stood among the huge trees in a long dress with a straw hat on her head and a hiking stick in her hand. At her neatly booted feet sat a basket and a bouquet. The woods were one big picnic fairyland for her, Mama always said. So different from Grandma Rendall, Daddy's mother, who hated the trees—couldn't get them cleared back from her house fast enough or far enough.

And here was Mama and Daddy's wedding picture. They looked so young and handsome, the two of them. And hopeful. They never knew hard times would come, or that one day they'd have a family and a forest fire would be heading toward them . . .

Patches threaded herself between Storie and the box.

"Mama, we'll take Patches, won't we? I mean, if we have to run for it? House pets are different from wild animals, right?"

"Of course."

Storie pulled Patches onto her lap and looked around, imagining the little shingled house engulfed in flames. Mama had tried to pretty it up with her red cretonne curtains and the doily strips she'd cut from newspapers and tacked along the shelves. But they didn't own the house. If it burned, it would be up to Sweetwater to replace it.

Storie wondered: Was it worse if you had more, because then you had more to lose? She'd seen pictures of living room sets in old copies of *Woman's World* magazine. That would be a lot of good furniture to burn up.

On the other hand, she didn't think of her home as just this cabin, this collection of fruit box furniture. Home, to her, took in a wider space, the forests and the mountains. If her home burned, it wouldn't be just this house, this shack. It would be her special place by the waterfall, it would be the view from the mountain behind camp. The best things couldn't be set on a flatcar.

Lifting Patches aside, she went out into the smoky yard and let herself into Snowflake's pen, gathering the little fawn into her arms. Lord, she didn't know whether to feel reassured that someone had finally given a thought to evacuating them, or scared that the fire had now come close enough that it might be necessary.

"Oh, Snowflake," she whispered. "What are we gonna do with you?"

A gainst the black night sky, bright flames shot up from the next ridge, lighting the bottoms of the roiling clouds an angry orange. Storie lay on her belly on the schoolhouse roof, arms hooked over the peak.

"Storie!" It was her brother. At first she didn't answer. "Storie, Mama's lookin' for you!"

"I'm up here."

"Hey, can you see the fire real good?"

"Yeah," she muttered. "Too good."

"Hey, you guys! Come on, let's get up on the roof!"

Swell, she thought, as the Staver boys materialized from the shadows. They climbed the leaning alder on the up side of the schoolhouse and dropped onto the roof. Now four sets of elbows hooked over the peak.

"Whoa," Sam said. "That there fire is coming to get us."

"It's like a monster," Johnny added.

"My mama says it's only three miles off," Billy said. "It could get here in no time."

In the quiet of that awful thought, they could actually hear the distant roar. Close up it must have been deafening. They were watching the surface of the earth being torn open, Storie thought, and from the huge pit all the forces of hell itself were erupting.

"Our dads are right in the middle of that," Johnny said.

There was a long silence.

"I wonder what it feels like, gettin' burned alive," Billy said.

"Oh, shut up!" Storie said.

"Sorry, Miss Priss. I forget we got a *lady* here we can't be scaring."

"You don't scare me. The fire scares me. Like it'd scare anybody with half a brain. I just don't see why you gotta put every ugly thought you ever had into words, that's all."

Again they watched in silence.

"My dad seen a blowup once," Sam said. "Fact he was practically in it. Says the air just exploded around him. All sorts of burnin' stuff whirlin' up like a tornado."

"Told us it was like death," Billy said. "Death by fire just a-comin' at you, chasin' you down."

After another pause, Johnny said, "One of them CCC boys got kilt today."

For the first time, Storie stopped staring at the fire. "Is that true?"

"I heard Mr. Wicks say so," Johnny answered.

Storie thought about Flynn Casey. And Daddy. Did his rule about a man only dying when his time came count for dying in fires too?

Oh, phooey, she thought, sliding down to the low eave and swinging off, dangling by her hands. She didn't care what Daddy said. People got killed when they had to do dangerous things, and forests were more likely to burn when people went out into them and got careless—no magic about any of it. She dropped the remaining few feet and landed in the dust.

Slapping her overalls, she scrambled down the hill. She didn't know how much she trusted what *anybody* said anymore. She'd been watching. She'd seen how all this went. They didn't know what that fire was going to do. And they expected her to lie there sleeping calm all night, confident she'd get plenty of warning if they had to run for it?

At home she went directly to the backyard, where she opened the fawn's pen and slipped in with her. Oh, Snowflake . . .

"There you are," Mama said from the back porch.

Storie whirled. "Daddy lied to me, Mama. He flat-out lied."

Mama came down the steps. "What are you talking about?"

"About the deer and all the animals. He said they just run away in a fire. Now I know that ain't true. They're out there gettin' burned up, right now."

Snowflake scampered in her pen like she understood why Storie was upset.

Mama sighed. "He hates to see you hurt, Storie. He says things like that because he wants to protect you."

"But he can't, can he? I'll find out everything sooner or later, and then it's just worse, 'cause he lied."

"Don't be too hard on him. It's only because he loves you."

"Love." She said it like a swearword. "Mama, whole herds a deer are dyin' out there—"

"Storie—"

"No, don't try to make me feel better, I know it's true. Probably thousands are dyin' and I got to get my heart tore out, worryin' over this one here. And why? Because I love her. So what exactly is the use of love? Just makes you scared of losin' what you got."

"Well, I know, but love's something that—

well, I don't know—without it, life just wouldn't be worth living."

Storie watched the fawn. That sounded right. That sounded like the way it was supposed to be. But at this moment, she couldn't feel it.

"I never should have saved her in the first place."

"Now don't talk like that. How were you supposed to know there'd be a fire? And she probably wouldn't have survived at all if you hadn't brought her home."

"Well, I've gotta let her go now. At least give her a chance."

"I guess you could, but, Storie, I still think they'll get the fire stopped. It's not that close."

"How can you *say* that?" Storie stared at her. "Mama, when you can see flames lickin' up in the black sky, to me that's close."

Her mother sighed and turned for the house.

Storie opened the pen's gate and stood aside. Snowflake edged up and nuzzled her.

"No, you're supposed to run for it." Oh, if this wasn't the most killing feeling—to have this little helpless creature trust you and look to you for care, and then not be able to do a thing to help it.

She stooped to put her arms around the fawn one more time.

"You ain't so helpless, Snowflake," she murmured. "You're strong now and you've grown more'n you know. You can run far and fast." She released the deer, stood and, leaving the pen open, backed toward the house. The deer trembled by the gate.

"Watch for cougars, hear? See if you can find you some big deer to follow." She reached for the door and then turned back. "Bye."

Inside, her mother was waiting, watching her with a worried expression.

"Oh, Mama," she burst out, "you just don't understand how I feel about that little thing."

"Oh, yes, I do," Mama said, enfolding her in her arms. "I certainly do."

It wasn't like Storie was a stranger to darkness, for there's nothing darker than a log camp on a starless winter night when the clouds hold the blackness right in close to the treetops. But this was a weird, unnatural darkness that made you fear the stars were gone forever.

Storie picked her way up the back path, wondering if Mama had somehow been mistaken. Could it really be morning?

She peered into Snowflake's pen. Empty.

Fallen wood ash lay like warm, dirty snow over everything, but Snowflake had left no prints. Good. Maybe she'd run off right after Storie'd opened the pen and was long gone to the west already. Storie stood there a moment, then followed her own newly laid footprints back to the porch.

What a long, strange, restless night it had been, knowing the fire was burning so nearby. Storie had lain awake, listening to the dry wind rattling along under the eaves, and slept only in brief snatches, dreaming of panicked deer herds bounding through the woods, and of trying to put out the fire by smothering it with hundreds of flapjacks. "Hurry," Wanda kept saying as the two of them hurled the floppy cakes onto the flames. "Flip 'em or they'll burn!"

Well, no flapjacks this morning. Her job had disappeared along with the men. Now she'd have Mama bossing her again.

She felt dry and empty; her nerves were brittle with the lack of sleep. She reached the porch and stood there, looking back. Although most of the wives and children were still here, the camp felt abandoned.

Jeannette Wicks had ended her summer stay early because of the smoke. May LaBranche had packed up and left too. It was her time, and this was sure no place to have a baby. Their teacher, Miss Fowler, had sent word she wouldn't be coming until all this settled down . . .

The birds. Suddenly Storie realized. Even the birds had gone. The bullfinches, the sparrows, the robins. No twittering through the trees, no flash of wing on the air.

She kept listening, but the silence was complete.

She opened the screen door. "Mama, you won't believe this, but the birds are gone."

Mama frowned. She came out to listen. "Maybe it's just the dark. Maybe they're confused and don't know it's morning."

"That don't figure, Mama. The birds usually start chirpin' around before the sun ever comes up."

Mama didn't meet her eyes. "I've seen it get dark like this during other fires."

"You ever see every last bird fly off?"

"Well, no," Mama admitted.

Someday, Storie thought, following her back inside, someday—times like this—I'll go when I think I ought to and stay only if I want.

Here it was, the hottest, smokiest day on earth and her mother had water heating on the woodstove, trying to get caught up on washing the grimy clothes Daddy had brought home from his first round of fire fighting.

She put Storie to work washing lamp chimneys and trimming wicks, a job that was taking even more time than usual now that they had to burn lamps at high noon just to do the house chores.

Johnny stuck his head in the back door. "Hey, your fawn's gone, Storie."

"I know. I set her free."

"What for? She's way too little. She'll never make it."

"She might. I think she will."

Storie hurried through the wick trimming, only to be handed a basket of mending.

"These are all things you can stitch up on the machine," Mama said.

"Mama! You expect me to sew on a day like this? We may have to run for it any minute."

"Well, if we have to, we will. But I can't see how standing there staring out the window is going to help put out the fire."

"Well, *I* can't see the use in mending things that might just get burned up."

"But they might not," Mama shot right back, "and then we'll be ahead on the mending."

Storie sighed. They would be ahead on *everything*. There was no keeping things clean, of course, with the air full of soot, but they'd probably never had the house better sorted out and patched up, thanks to Mama's keep busy plan.

"Be the tidiest house ever burned up," Storie muttered.

"What's that, young lady?"

"I'm going down to Sam and Billy's," Johnny said.

"Oh no you don't." Mama put her fists on her hips. "You stay right around the yard."

"Aw gee, do I hafta?"

"Yes. I don't want you taking off. Just in case."

"In case what?"

"In case we have to jump on the train, what do you think?" Storie said. "You forgettin' the whole forest is burnin' up out there?"

"I ain't a-scared."

"Well, goody for you. Be scared or don't be scared, who cares? Just be ready to get on the train."

"Storie!" Mama said. "I'm starting to think you're a little out of your head with this."

And you're not? Storie wanted to say. Looked to her like everybody had their own way of going crazy. She was starting to wonder if her mother's idea of staying fixed on the little things meant she was the sort of woman who'd die trying to save a couple of jars of canned fruit. She'd be caught in her tracks, still busy pretending everything was going to be okay.

Johnny slouched out the door, pouting. Storie didn't feel one bit sorry for him. Nobody was chaining him to a sewing machine.

"I'm sorry, Mama, but it does make me antsy, sittin' here gettin' ourselves buried in ashes, just waitin' for somebody to tell us what we should do."

"I know you're scared, Storie. But just remember, we've got all our men out there standing between us and that fire."

"Hey, you know what? I'd rather be out there fightin' that fire with 'em than stuck here waitin' for it."

"Estora Faye, for shame!"

"I mean it," Storie said. "When I was up there working at the cookhouse, at least I felt like part of the fight. But *this* . . . like we don't have eyes to see the fire coming or brains to run like the animals . . ."

"But to make light of the fire fighting—"

"I ain't makin' light of it. It's you who's makin' light of what we're doin' here."

"But we're not doing anything—"

"We're tryin' to act like this is a normal day, for cryin' out loud. Just as hard, in its own way."

"Your hair's not getting singed, is it? Your hands aren't blistered. So I don't like to hear you talk like this while those men are out there trying to protect you—"

"Protectin' me? Come again! They're savin' the trees so they can cut 'em down later."

"Storie!"

"And Mrs. Wicks packed up and left. Why can't we? If Daddy wants us protected, why don't he just send us down to Grandma's farm? Ever think of that?"

Mama looked startled, her face pinched in a way that made Storie wonder if she'd hit on some little part of a painful truth.

Then Mama spoke with a great effort at calm, and what she said took Storie by surprise. "It's not your father's fault the woods are on fire."

"Mama. I know that."

"Do you?"

"Well, of course. The forest's on fire because it's hot and dry and people weren't careful enough."

"But you're not mad at them. You're mad at your father."

Storie turned away.

Maybe I am, she thought, because a few minutes later when a speeder pulled into Blue Star bearing a load of soot-blackened loggers that included her father, she hung back. She didn't join the wives and children who went out on the tracks to meet the men, all of whom seem to be headed for the family end of camp.

Hanging on the porch post, she nodded at her father as he went inside.

"So where's the rest of 'em?" she whispered to her mother. For the first time, her father home safe wasn't enough. She wanted Flynn Casey safe too. It would be a shame if she didn't get to hear just exactly what shocking thing he might say to her next.

Mama studied her with new interest. "Still on the lines, he says. They only sent back the men with families." She smiled faintly. "Guess that's why they call them the homeguard."

The men had been fed at the fire camp and they'd dozed on the train. Now they'd been ordered to build a firebreak between the fire and Blue Star, heave up some last-minute protective dirt embankments around the steam donkey down on the lower side.

"How bad is it, Daddy?" Storie asked when he came back out.

"Well, you can forget the Yacolt." He stopped on the ditch plank and squinted south. "Now on, folks talk big fires, they'll be talkin' about the Tillamook."

The ocean, Flynn Casey thought, verging on delirium. *God be praised! The ocean's come to put out the fire.* For the sound of a mighty forest succumbing to flames is like the thundering of a thousand waves crashing upon the shore.

His eyeballs felt swollen to bursting. And his lungs—the air seared his nostrils, his throat and right down to his insides, which screamed for cool and fresh but got only dry and burning. His shovel was fused to his raw palms with caked blood.

"Casey!" Someone shook him, hard. "Run, man! This way."

As he topped the ridge and headed blindly downhill, his empty canteen banging against his thigh, he was aware of other crew members scrambling through the steep tangle of cutover hillside some distance from him. Once he glanced back over his shoulder, saw tongues of flame flaring over the ridge. Crowning. Oh, Christ, crowning everyplace there was standing timber for the fire to race up. They were barreling down a hillside directly in the fire's path.

The stream, the one hope. If only the downhill slowing of the fire gave them enough time. He half fell toward the draw, stopping to climb a deadfall, then threw himself forward again through the ankle-grabbing slash. At last he reached the water and stumbled, splashing, up the rocky streambed to a pool. He plunged gratefully into the coolness, gulping great drafts of the precious stuff. He couldn't get enough as every dried-out cell in his body cried for water. He came up sputtering, shaking his head, his mind cleared and suddenly filled with the fresh notion that he might live through this after all. With cupped hands he tossed water over the moss-covered log that formed the pool, then pulled out his bandanna for a mask.

The crackling fire had slowed on the downhill advance, making it torture to crouch in the water when his every instinct was to climb out and run, get away, put quick distance between himself and those flames. But *Hold on, hold on,* he kept telling himself. He might be a young hothead, but he was smart enough to know when to listen to the old-timers, and they'd warned that a fire could leap a creek and tear uphill with a speed that couldn't be outrun. Weren't the slopes of these mountains already littered with the carcasses of the panicky creatures who'd tried it and failed?

But to huddle there, watching it coming . . . hearing it . . . Oh, for wings like the birds, long flown. God. Someone had to warn them up at Blue Star. A devil wind for certain, shifting north like this, and the speed of this thing . . . the women and children. He flashed on a picture of that blond girl, Rendall's daughter . . . Estora. Storie. Sure someone would phone the camp . . . But phone lines were burning through all over the place. He gulped air and went down again. Blessed coolness, water of life . . .

When he came up, the fire was almost upon him. He caught sight of another man up the stream. Looked like he'd found a decent-sized puddle. Good.

In the other direction he was surprised to meet the eyes of a young doe, a blacktail, who'd joined him in the pool with her frightened fawn.

It'll not be long now, he thought, eyes smarting as he watched the fire thundering down on them like a freight train at full throttle. Then he stared in wonder as a tawny cougar slipped into the pool on his other side. The strangeness of it—

longtime enemies crouching together in a pool so small they could almost touch. But now the fire itself commanded every terrified heartbeat.

And then the conflagration was over them, heating the water, sucking away the air. Flynn held himself under by bracing against the log until at last he was forced to come up gasping. As he broke the water's surface, his ears were filled with an unearthly roar, his lungs assaulted by a blast of heat. Hellfire on earth. *Hail Mary, Mother of God . . .*

Storie stuffed the quilt into the washtub,
punching down the ballooning layers of fabric.

"Get a ladder or a barrel or something to
stand on," she called to Johnny. "Let's get this up
on the roof."

Pushing up from the overturned rain barrel
he brought, she clambered over the eave. Mama
and Johnny together struggled to lift the wet quilt
toward her. She dragged it over the shingled edge,
wincing at the rough treatment she was giving the
soft cotton fabric and tiny, careful stitching. Well,
Grandma sure wouldn't want them to sit here and

burn up out of respect for her handiwork. Scooting along on her rear, Storie spread it over a section of the roof, covering dried moss, fir needles and ashes.

Lord, it was hot. Hotter'n hollerin' hell. She twisted around, squinting to the east. Thick smoke. You could feel the fire out there; you could hear it.

"Mama, I think it's coming."

"Get down from there then! Oh, dear, I wonder how close it is to Tom and the others."

"Where *are* they?"

"Down on that lower spur. Oh, Lord . . ."

Uproar filled the family end of camp. Every water tap ran wide open as women soaked anything they could get their hands on. Kids old enough to help heaved their families' belongings onto the flatcars. No official evacuation order had been given, but what else could people think?

A frantic chorus of squeals announced the panicked stampeding of a half dozen hogs. The littlest children sent up howls of their own as the animals charged through camp.

Storie looked at her mother. Did she realize what this meant? Bridey wouldn't open the hog pen unless she was convinced it was all over for Blue Star.

"Mama," Johnny said, "Stavers are digging a hole out back to bury stuff and save it from the fire. Want me to do that?"

· "No, anything worth saving we'll take on the train," Mama said.

A simultaneous cry of dismay echoed up and down the row. The water taps had run dry.

"Prob'ly just the pressure," Alice called. "Maybe we gotta take turns."

"What about a bucket brigade from the creek?" Mavis Bunch suggested.

Mrs. Potter picked up her little girl. "Comes to that, maybe we ought to just run down to the swimming hole and dunk under."

Mrs. Staver swung two cages of squawking chickens onto a flatcar. "What the hell is this damn train parked here for if it ain't takin' us out when we need it? That's what I'd like to know. We're supposed to risk our skins wettin' down these lousy shacks? I say somebody ought to go up and tell Wicks to fire up the shay this minute!" She looked straight at Mama as she said this.

"Ethel," Mama said to Mrs. Staver, "I'm with you. I've argued against panicking, but now I'd say we've cut this close enough."

"Ain't us doin' the cuttin', is it? I'd've vamoosed days ago."

But as Mama turned to head for the office, Mr. Wicks came puffing down the tracks, Mr. Clinkinbeard hot on his heels. "This is it!" Mr. Wicks yelled. "Let's haul freight!"

"Well, heaven be praised," Mrs. Staver muttered sarcastically.

"We just lost our water line. Burnin' tree fell right over it."

The women stared at each other.

"Camp Six is gone," Mr. Wicks went on. "The wooden dam at Rock Creek burned up, let the whole log pond loose."

Mr. Clinkinbeard set a valise and his caged mynah onto a flatcar. "Let's go. I had a call at the office, said trestles are burning."

"Trestles *we* gotta go over?" Mrs. Staver demanded.

"Can't say. The line went dead. Let's get out of here."

"Yep," Mr. Wicks said. "Load her up."

"But what about the men?" Mama asked.

Mr. Wicks was hurrying away. "We'll leave 'em a speeder, Margie."

"Wait! You're not sending someone to fetch them?"

He stopped and turned back. "They'll come. When they see it's hopeless, they'll give it up."

Mama sucked in a shocked breath, then followed a few steps. "Oh no you don't. If I know my Tom, he'll drop in his tracks out there, defending some old donkey engine, if that's what you told him to do."

Daddy. "You ain't thinkin' of leavin' my daddy down there," Storie said.

Mr. Wicks went red to his ears as he glanced from one accusing face to another.

"Uh, maybe we can pick 'em up on the way."

"Maybe?" Mama said. *"Maybe?"*

"Listen here, Margie. The wind's shifted and the fire's coming. You want me to sit here with a load of women and children or you want me to get you out?"

"Since when do *you* drive the train?" Mama said. "We could leave fine without you. So if you think leaving a speeder for our men is good enough, I say you can jolly well stay here with it."

"Margie's right!" Mrs. Staver said. "You're the one ought to hustle your fat fanny down that hill. You sent our men down there—you go get 'em back!"

"Take the speeder," Mama said.

"Oh, look, they'll be back up here before I could even bring it around." Beads of sweat popped out on his forehead. "We don't have time."

In that hot, suspended instant, Storie saw that shaming the superintendent was useless. The man couldn't move fast enough to do any of them any good. If he went down there, speeder or no, he'd probably have a heart attack and the crew would be stuck with lugging him back.

"I'll go," Storie said, and lit out through camp before anyone could stop her.

"Storie!" she heard her mother cry. She didn't answer. Heck, she'd be back before they were done arguing.

"Daddy!" she yelled, turning down the spur line that curved into the main tracks past the cookhouse. "Daddy!" He could never hear her from here, she knew, but she felt like yelling it anyway, because suddenly all that business about learning to cook and reading books and growing up . . . all that just fell away. Her father was down there and she had to get him back.

She pounded down the tracks, her lungs burning. She could hear the fire, a gnawing roar. When she rounded a curve expecting to find the men and didn't, her chest seized.

What if they'd cut straight up the hill someplace else and missed her? She'd be running down into the fire while they were getting away.

No, they had to be down here. Like Mama said, Daddy'd stick with Sweetwater's equipment way beyond what the company deserved. She kept going, over the creek trestle, slats of daylight flying by under her feet. It felt good, in the strangest way, to push her body, to run, to try, to put all her love and fear into motion.

"Daddy!" But the fire whirled up a din and the trees cracked and boomed. Faintly, above the rumbling, the camp's fire whistle wailed.

Finally, on the second switchback, silhouetted against flames burning in a cutover, she saw them.

"Daddy!" She yelled so hard her head ached. He couldn't have heard her, but almost as if he felt her there, he turned.

She saw his grip on his shovel relax in surprise. He glanced at the other men, who stopped and turned too, but only briefly. A man can't turn his back for long on a wall of fire like that.

She jumped up and down, waving her arms, motioning them up the hill, then stopped, watching for their reaction.

Oh, thank God. They were coming, stumbling up the tracks toward her as she stood there, panting, trying to catch her breath in the blistering air.

"Storie Faye, my God," Daddy said, hurtling past her, grabbing her on the way, "I'll kill the lamebrain sent you down here."

"Sent myself, Daddy," she huffed. "We're leaving. Everybody. We gotta get on the train."

"Give up the camp?"

"Got to. Water's out."

Stunned, the men stopped.

"Well, I'll be . . . ," somebody muttered, and they exchanged disgusted glances from red-rimmed eyes. "Nice a them to let us know."

Shovels dropped to the rail ties.

"Come on!" Daddy grabbed Storie's arm again.

Boom! The ground shook. *Boom boom!* Up past camp a cloud rose and swirled with debris.

"Daddy! What was—"

"Boom!"

"Dynamite shack!" Rex hollered. "Spark musta hit it!"

Daddy could hardly talk. "Your mama and Johnny—on the train?"

She nodded, suddenly exhausted now that her message was delivered. Climbing back up this grade was ten times as hard as flying down.

"Come on, peewee. We gotta highball."

Storie tried to double-time it, but it was like being pulled along by a big strong machine, a soot-covered human steam lokey. Tired as he was, Daddy had a grip on her that wouldn't let go. Her knees ached with pumping, her lips cracked with gasping in the blast-furnace air. Couldn't they rest, just for a moment? But no, the train might not wait. A roar filled her head. Was it the fire or her own blood, rushing in her ears? Her father kept slapping at her, trying to bare-handedly smother the flying sparks landing on her.

"There it is," somebody hollered, and Storie raised her scorching eyeballs to see the train rolling slowly, tentatively by the spur junction. Storie saw someone—her mother—jump up. She was waving her arms to signal the engineer, waving at them to hurry.

Storie felt the fire's heat at her back and heard the frantic encouragement from the families on the flatcars. A final surge of strength charged through her limbs as she and the men staggered toward the train.

And then arms were pulling her upward.

"Storie!" Her mother's eyes were streaming with relief and rage. "You scared me to death!"

Mama was hugging her, hugging Daddy, hugging Johnny. They were all of them holding each other and collapsing into a huddle in the center of the flatcar.

As the last exhausted man was hauled aboard, the train lurched forward, the whistle sounding low and mournful. Storie felt Mama's grip tighten on her arm.

"Stay in the middle," Mama said, trying to hold her whole family in her arms at once.

Storie lay panting, washed with relief. Whatever happened now, they were together. And no matter what the train had to go through, at least she didn't have to run. She could rest.

"*Awwk!*" cried the mynah. "How's she loggin'? How's she loggin'?"

Storie sat up. "Patches!" She patted the piles and boxes around her. "Where is she?"

"We couldn't find her," Mama said.

"She's not on the train?"

"I'm sorry, honey."

Storie sank back down.

Mama fumbled around and handed her a yellow wad. "Here. Your dress. I wet it down for you."

Storie spread it over her head.

Burning embers were dropping into the camp as they pulled away. In her last glimpse before they careened down the mountain, she saw flames shooting up from the schoolhouse set against the hill.

Boom! More dynamite.

"Hang on tight, peewee," Daddy said as the train gathered speed.

She nestled against him, her teeth banging together so hard she thought they'd break right out of her head. These rickety rails weren't built for trains to outrun danger.

The shay thundered down steep grades, wrenched against sharp canyon cuts. In places trees flamed on both sides of the tracks and smoke welled up from beneath the many trestles. Storie clung to her father, watching the cliff sides whiz by until she had to shut her eyes for the whirling dust and cinders.

At the curve above Ripple Creek Storie squinted back from the one spot that usually afforded a clear view of Blue Star Camp's mountainside perch. But everything was lost in smoke. She'd already had her last glimpse of Blue Star without even knowing it.

The secret pool, the little garden spot, the cool water and the brown trout. Cinders. And what about Snowflake? The baby owl? Patches . . . And then, with a stab, oh, Flynn . . .

A hot spark zinged her cheek. She slapped it, ducking back down. Time later to tote up all that was gone. For now they could only hang on tight to this wild ride that was taking them faster than any of them were prepared to go, away from the only life they'd ever known.

WIND TURNS FIRE
FROM TILLAMOOK

WESTWARD SWEEP HALTS
IN NORTHWEST BREEZE

HEAVY SMOKE PALL
COVERS PORTLAND

From the Sunday *Oregonian*
August 27, 1933

In the silence of the ghostly landscape, the black bear searched for her lost cub. From the cool, shrouding clouds, rain fell into the warm cinders of what had once been a mighty forest. Venturing out onto a flat rock at the edge of a waterfall pool, the bear dipped in a tentative paw, then quickly pulled it back. No dinner here. The water wasn't right. Trout floated, white bellies skyward, in a warm, ashy sludge.

Death by fire—the smell was everywhere. An entire herd of deer lay charred where they'd fallen in flight, their faces pointed west, toward safety.

One doe, blinded by fear and smoke, had leapt with such force that she had impaled herself on the branch of a downed tree.

Nosing along, the bear uncovered smaller tragedies as well. Every nest, every burrow had its own silent story of loss.

The bear could find not one familiar smell. The world itself had been utterly transformed, shades of green to shades of gray. Bewildered, she wandered on through the wasteland.

The eighth-grade boys in Forest Grove hung back from the new girl, she looked so grownup and solemn. The bolder of the high-school boys who spotted her walking the hilly streets in the afternoons wasted no time checking her out, but they found her answers flat, never flirty, and she had a way of looking directly into their eyes that made the most confident of them shrink.

"Wanna go for a Coke?" one would say. Missing the point, she'd answer, "Sorry, I don't drink Coke." And that would be that.

The flurry of interest had died away by the time the leaves were falling.

Fine by Storie. None of them had quite the right combination of curly dark hair and ruddy cheeks she had come to feel was exactly right; none of them seemed at all likely to spark things up by quoting interesting poetry at her.

A classmate or two asked about the fire, but with only the mildest curiosity. These were town kids, after all. The fire to them had been mainly a matter of a few smoky days in August. They would not truly understand about the forest until they went out for their first picnics next spring.

But Storie was haunted by the loss, and often in school she sat staring out the window at the heavy dark clouds rolling in over Gales Peak, imagining the ashy slopes that lay beyond.

Not that living in town was so bad. She was still a bit dazed at finding herself in this big red-brick building with an entire class just for eighth-graders, but who'd complain about having indoor plumbing or being able to flick a switch to turn on the lights?

At her grandmother's place she had a room of her own and, at Grandma's insistence, new clothes in the closet, some from the store, some home-made. For her fourteenth birthday Grandma had given her a little party, inviting a few neighbors. Storie couldn't get over it when details of this event were actually published in the local weekly alongside other stories of who was visiting folks in town and who'd been sick.

Johnny was making friends quickly, winning instant attention for his daredeviling antics, and of course Mama's main problem was simply hiding her pleasure at being in town. That wouldn't do at all, with Daddy so beaten down about it. She told Storie she almost felt guilty, having the fire decide things her way. Daddy couldn't very well argue in favor of a way of life that had burned up.

Poor Daddy, Storie often thought. He hardly seemed his old self around Grandma's. It helped that Uncle Ralph had gone off to a railroad job, leaving Daddy with plenty to do in the way of chores in the vegetable garden and orchard. But he worked so hard at keeping busy, he was in danger of catching up completely. Then what would he do? Already he'd split enough firewood for three winters.

Mama understood that Daddy needed to be head of his own house, and she had her eye on a cottage that a neighboring widow wanted to rent partly in exchange for some help around her place. But that seemed to be out of the question until Daddy had real work again.

For Storie, of course, whatever else happened, town life offered the solace of books. Books at the school and books at the library, which she walked right by every day on her way home. She found on its shelves a fat volume of poetry, one where you could look up any poem, just from its first line.

O Western wind, when wilt thou blow
That the small rain down can rain
Christ, that my love were in my arms . . .

She thought often of Flynn. She'd never seen
him after the fire, but if he'd been killed, she figured she'd have read it in the papers, like she read
about the one CCC boy who did die.

Fire stories circulated for weeks among the
displaced. Tales were told of ashes falling on ships
five hundred miles out to sea and piling a foot deep
on the beaches. People recounted their narrow es-
capes and shared the relief that fire crews thought
lost were found safe.

Once, in the hardware store, Storie overheard her father telling someone how they'd
been burned out of Blue Star. He didn't realize
she was standing in earshot when he finished by
describing how she'd come flying down the grade
to warn them. "Weren't for that gal a mine, we'd
a been toast."

He never mentioned Mr. Wicks's questionable
judgment, though, or complained of how the company had let risk their lives.

"That's just your father's way," Mama told
Storie when she pointed it out. "And besides, that
sort of thing happens all the time."

"But shouldn't Mr. Wicks be punished?" Storie
asked.

Mama shrugged. "He has to live with himself.
Maybe that's punishment enough."

*   *   *

FOR THOSE WHOSE lives were inextricably linked
with the forest, it was a gloomy fall of counting the
losses—eleven billion board feet of timber, the local paper reported, equal to all the timber cut in
the United States in the previous year. Two hundred and forty thousand acres burned, an area
half the size of the state of Rhode Island. One
newspaper article called it the most destructive
forest blaze in modern times.

But before long, interesting reports began to
come back with those who'd ventured out to assess
the damage in the blackened forest. The trees had
been killed, certainly, and the forest was dead. But
these were huge trees with thick bark. Under the
charred outer crust of the giants was hidden good,
solid wood. Much could be salvaged if the loggers
could beat the insects to it.

The massive trunks were still warm when the
companies patched together their operations and
returned to the ashy skeleton forest.

Storie would never forget Daddy coming home
from his first day back logging, black from head to
foot, his eyeballs startlingly white.

"Tom!" Mama's hand flew to her mouth. "Why,
you look like a coal miner."

"Get used to it," he said.

Gone was the fragrance of the woods Storie
had always loved on him. Never again would he
carry in that fresh scent.

"Still as death out there," he said. "No animals. No sounds. Nothing. Just the wind." He shrugged out of his mackinaw. "There's sound timber, though. There's work. Work for years."

"Really?" Mama couldn't help letting her face brighten a bit. "Think we could rent Mrs. Epley's little house, then?"

"Don't know why not," Daddy said. "I figure we could swing it right after Christmas." Then he turned to Storie. "Say, guess who showed up on the job today. Asked about you too. Young Flynn Casey."

THE DOORBELL RANG on a dark December night of torrential rain. It hadn't rained like this since 1896, reports were saying. Gales Creek and the other streams were flooding with muddy runoff from the denuded mountainsides.

Mama had gone over to the widow's house, and it was Storie who flicked on the porch light and opened the door.

"Flynn!"

"Hello, Storie." There he stood, rain running down into his collar, his dark eyes twinkling as dangerously as ever.

She glanced over her shoulder, half expecting Daddy to come charging out.

"Don't worry," Flynn said. "He's given me permission."

"Permission?"

Flynn grinned. "To come callin' on you, a course. What did you think?"

Storie blushed the blush of her life. "Well," she said. "Well."

"Who's at the door?" Grandma called, bustling out.

"Flynn. Flynn Casey from Blue Star Camp. You know, before."

"Oh. Well, don't keep him outside," Grandma said, although this seemed more to do with good manners than with any real warmth. Her look as she headed back for the kitchen was as cool as the draft that blew in with him.

Flynn pulled off his cap, shook the rain out and stepped inside. "We *were* longing for rain," he said, picking up the conversation right where they'd left off four months earlier.

"Right," Storie said, smiling shyly, remembering the poem. "But *small* rain, wasn't that it?"

He must have remembered it too because suddenly they were grinning at each other in a way that had nothing to do with the fire or with the rain and everything to do with the simple rightness of him finally being here.

Her father chose this moment to make his presence felt in the kitchen doorway. He crossed his arms over his chest and nodded. "Flynn."

"Tom."

Her father hesitated, taking his time, giving them each a long, stern look. Then he went back into the kitchen.

Storie widened her eyes at Flynn.

Flynn looked around the cozy room, taking in the trimmed Christmas tree, the crackling fire. "Fine fire you've got going."

"You better come sit by it," she said. "You're soaked."

They pulled chairs up to the cheerful blaze.

"So tell me what happened to you," Storie said. "In the fire, I mean. I've wondered and wondered."

He smiled. "Have you, now? Well, I don't mind tellin' it, although I'm hopin' never again to have to live such a thing . . ."

As FLYNN BEGAN to spin out his tale, Storie's grandmother fussed at her father in the kitchen.

"You shouldn't even let this get started," she whispered. "Just when she's finally down here and has a chance of meeting all sorts of fine young men . . ."

Storie's father turned from the crack in the kitchen door. "In the first place," he said, "I have the feeling it's already started."

His mother-in-law joined him to squint at the slice of parlor view revealing two heads—one blond, one dark—tilting toward each other against the glowing firelight.

"Hmm," she mumbled. "I believe you're right. Well . . ." She went back to fixing the obligatory tray of cookies and hot chocolate.

"And as for meeting your fine young town fellas, hey, the girl could do worse." He hooked his
thumbs in his suspenders. "After all, Maude, the
boy *is* a logger."

"**G**ramma Storie?" Katie said. "Isn't that log camp where you lived when you were a kid out here somewhere?"

"Must be." Estora gazed across the staggered rows of ridges, shades of green receding into distant blues. They were on their way to the coast for Mother's Day weekend—Estora with her son, Richard, his wife, Marsha, and their two children. They had stopped for the moment at Richard's favorite Sunset Highway viewpoint.

"So could we go there sometime?" Katie asked. "To Blue Star Camp?"

"Oh, honey, your Grampa Flynn and I looked for it years ago, and even then we weren't sure we were in the right spot. It'd be completely overgrown by now."

"Yes," Richard said. "Isn't it just amazing to see all that green? When you think how it was before? I still remember every trip to the coast when I was a kid, driving through mile after mile of it—nothing but bleached-out snags. The ghost forest, we called it."

Eleven-year-old Tom spoke to Estora from the corner of his mouth. "He says this every time we stop here."

Estora smiled. Her son, the forester. Her father had never gotten over her becoming a teacher, and if he wasn't already gone, he'd sure drop dead now to find he had a grandson who not only had gone to college but had turned into a fern stomper down at that forestry school to boot.

It hadn't surprised her, though. Seemed like the whole family was born to a love of the forest, whatever way they showed it.

"You kids probably can't even begin to imagine what this looked like after the fires, right, Mom?"

Estora shrugged. Maybe they could. Some people were better at imagining than others.

"You know, I was trying to figure it out the other day," Richard said, "which fire Uncle John fought. Wasn't the one in forty-five, was it?"

"No, because in 1945 Johnny was on a troop ship to Japan. Must have been the fire of thirty-nine. He was just a kid—sixteen or so."

"Is that Uncle Johnny Logger you're talking about?" Tom asked.

"That's right," Marsha said. "The one you met at the family reunion in Vernonia that time?"

"Oh, yeah," Tom said. "Hey, remember that one kid who climbed way up a tree and all the moms were yelling at him to get down?"

Marsha lifted an eyebrow. "The Rendall cousins made quite an impression on them."

Estora smiled. They were a wild bunch all right, the Rendalls. Came by it honestly too.

"Anyway," Richard continued, "these mountains burned so many times there wasn't a seed cone left for miles around—no hope of the forest ever reseeding itself. So just think of the incredible challenge of it—a reforestation project never tried on this scale before. And you kids should be proud, because it was the people of Oregon who forked over the money to do it. And pitched in to plant some of the trees too. I remember doing it myself. Seventh grade I think it was."

Probably every kid who grew up in this corner of Oregon could claim a few of those young trees, Estora thought. How well she remembered the science-class field trips her three kids had gone on, the special lunch boxes she'd packed. "Mom!" her daughter, Jane, had protested. "You packed enough food for a whole logging crew!" Well, old habits died hard.

"But I'd like to see some of those really big trees," Katie said now. "Like in pictures, where people made little cabins inside just one trunk? Or, you know, Daddy, that one on the piano of Great-great Grandma with her long skirt and hiking stick. And she looks like a doll or something standing by that big tree?"

"Geez, Katie," Tom said. "Those trees are history. Don't you know that?"

"Tom." Marsha put her hand on Katie's shoulder.

"But think of the *new* trees, honey," Richard said. "Isn't it kind of exciting how we're always learning new ways of taking care of the forests? Even our ideas about fire have changed. Some people even think we ought to start having prescribed burns."

"You mean set fires on purpose?" Katie said.

"That's right, to clear out the undergrowth so the fuel doesn't build up. And of course nowadays we've learned we can get more wood in the long run by cutting the trees in sixty years or so, then starting over."

Katie frowned. "So there'll never be really big trees again?"

"Sweetheart," Richard said, "you have to think of trees as a crop. You wouldn't let a crop sit out in a field to rot, would you? Of course not. You want to harvest at the optimum time."

Katie set her eight-year-old face hard, and Estora could tell she was struggling with a feeling she remembered herself all too well—that of knowing in your heart there is something not quite right, or at least not complete about an argument, but not being immediately able to figure out what's been left unsaid.

"Still," Katie persisted, "I think there should be some big ones."

"There's still a few," Marsha said, "tucked here and there."

"Yes." Estora couldn't resist. "And there are folks who'd love to take their chain saws to those too."

Katie's blond head whipped around in alarm.

"Now, Mom," Richard said. "Let's not get going on that again."

The Caseys all loved the trees. The Rendalls too. That didn't mean they all *agreed* about the trees.

"Tell you what," Richard said, obviously trying to be conciliatory, "let's stop at the giant Sitka spruce. It's just before we get to the beach. I'll bet Katie would like that."

Estora nodded, privately depressed at the thought. Once when she and Flynn had stopped at the wayside park honoring the biggest tree in Oregon, a full trash can had been tipped over and litter was drifting against the massive tree's roots. Slightly pathetic somehow, this lone forest giant, rising from the garbage.

They'd felt much the same dismay two years ago when they'd taken a plane trip to California just before Flynn died. *Thick as the hair on a dog's back*, they used to say of the trees in Oregon's forests. But from the air, the mountains today brought to mind a dog with mange.

Oh Daddy, she'd thought, her forehead pressed against the plane's window. Oh Daddy, swinging your lunch pail down the tracks, home from another day's work in the big woods. If you could have seen this, *then* would you have believed it wouldn't last forever?

Imagining. Some people had trouble with it. People like her father, who could look at a great expanse of forest and simply refuse to believe that it could ever be gone.

But being able to imagine was everything. Take these trees in front of them now. They wouldn't *be* here if at least a few people hadn't been able to look at those silent, windswept slopes fifty years ago and picture them green again in the future. Imagining things better and then starting on it. Why was it so hard?

Now she rested a hand on Katie's shoulder and looked out over that sea of hopeful new green. Somewhere beyond the second ridge was her own little plot of mixed evergreens, her tree farm on Silver Creek. Well, she called it a farm to keep her son happy, but nobody was going to clear-cut *that* twenty-five acres like a crop. Not while she was still kicking.

Every winter she went out with her shovel and canvas bag of seedlings to stick in a few more. It just bothered her, she told the kids, seeing a bare spot that ought to have a tree and didn't. And the funny thing was, in all the years she'd lived, she'd never found anything she could do with greater conviction or more back-aching satisfaction than planting those trees.

"Isn't it true," Katie said with a sidelong look at her father, "that certain animals and birds like the really old, big trees best?"

Estora glanced at her son, suppressing a smile at his fumbling answer. He'd be busy these next years, trying to keep up with this granddaughter of hers.

And wasn't that a comfort, she thought, knowing the world had Katie—Katie and all the other young ones out there with their relentless wondering about things?

"Gramma Storie," Katie said as they headed back for the minivan, "tell your story about the fire again, will you?"

"The whole thing?" Estora climbed into the van. "Or you just want the part about the ranger finding my cat alive?"

Katie scooted in beside her. "The whole thing."

"Okay, you're the boss . . ."

Richard pulled the van out onto the highway.

"I'll never forget the day it started," Estora

began, "because it was the day my brother Johnny ran the trestle."

"That's Uncle John, that we were talking about before?"

"That's right. Anyway, it was hot. Hotter'n hollerin' hell."

"Mom, please!"

Estora leaned forward. "Now you listen here. I gave up saying 'ain't' years and years ago, but some woods words are just exactly right, and if Katie wants me to talk about that fire, then 'hotter'n hollerin' hell' is something I just have to say."

Richard hunched his shoulders. "Okay, sorry."

"They hear worse all the time on the tube," Marsha pointed out. "Go on."

"Well, it was what they used to call a fire-in-the-sky day," Estora began again, "with that east wind the old-timers all dreaded . . ."

Katie leaned against her grandmother, listening and imagining, as, outside the van window, the young green trees flashed past.

AFTERWORD

With the exception of President Roosevelt, all the named characters in this story are fictional, as is the Blue Star Camp of the Sweetwater Timber Company. The Tillamook Burn of 1933, however, occurred as described.

ABOUT THE AUTHOR

LINDA CREW is a fourth-generation Oregonian whose great-great-grandmother arrived in the 1860s by way of the Oregon Trail. Linda Crew was born and brought up in Corvallis, where she now lives on Wake Robin Farm with her husband, Herb, and their children, Miles, Mary, and William. Her other books are *Nekomah Creek,* an ALA Notable Book; *Nekomah Creek Christmas; Someday I'll Laugh About This;* and *Children of the River,* which won the International Reading Association Children's Book Award for 1990 in the Older Reader Category, was chosen as a Best Book for Young Adults by the American Library Association, and was the 1989 Honor Book for the Golden Kite Award given by the Society of Children's Book Writers.